APR 0 9 2013

SURFACING

SURFACING

NORA RALEIGH BASKIN

CANDLEWICK PRESS

Copyright © 2012 by Nora Raleigh Baskin

First edition 2012

Library of Congress Catalog Card Number 2012942396
ISBN 978-0-7636-4908-1

12 13 14 15 16 17 BVG 10 9 8 7 6 5 4 3 2 1
Printed in Berryville, VA, U.S.A.

This book was typeset in Berkeley Oldstyle.

Candlewick Press
99 Dover Street
Somerville, Massachusetts 02144

visit us at www.candlewick.com

For my brother, Stephen, with whom I share,
not this exact story, but this truth.

Leah

*The most peaceful memory I have is of when I drown.
And if I close my eyes, I can still see the sunlight, cut
into white bands, broken at the water's surface. Beyond
that, far above that, is the sky, blue and dotted white
with clouds that seem to float in a mirror image of the
water in which I am submerged. The burning pain of
my first underwater breath is gone. Now when I inhale
again, it is a warm and lovely feeling.*

*I wasn't supposed to swim across the pool to the deep
end. I wasn't supposed to be in the pool at all. But it
was so hot and the water looked so good, cool and wet,
and blue. There was the slide across the way, baking
white in the heat. I can make it, I thought. I can paddle
and kick, and I do. Then suddenly I am so tired, so very
tired.*

I surface again.

I can see the people sitting around the deck, even though my head is barely above the surface now. There is an old couple sitting at one of the plastic tables, under an umbrella, playing cards. A teenager and his summer girlfriend are lying in the sun, their chairs pulled back onto the grass, far from the concrete surrounding the pool. And that one little girl, but now all I can see are the imprints of her feet on the concrete, already drying in the sun.

Help. I call out, "Help," but no one looks up. No one hears me. My voice is too little, a watery whisper, and then I go under again.

It is a long-ago instinct to hold my breath under the water, but very soon my lungs start to squeeze in pain as the air runs out. And without my brain explaining how or why, my arms pull and my legs push and one more time I pop back up.

Ah, my mouth opens, air rushes inside, and the pain is gone. It is gone.

I want to call out again. Help me. Please, somebody help me. The little girl has gone. The old lady playing cards is opening a can of soda now. The teenage couple is kissing, but I am too tired. I am more tired than I have ever been in my nine years. The teenagers *are kissing, and I know now that I will never be kissed like that.*

This time when I go under, I don't fight. I let the water cover my face and the top of my head. I look up at the sky, the white clouds, the absolute beauty of sunlight making its way through the water as if nothing can stop it. I can see the surface of the water and then the blur of what lies past that, distorted, but in a way more clear than anything I have ever seen. A weariness takes over my body, and I surrender to it.

One

When practice was over, most of the girls, like Maggie, had thrown on their sweatpants or pajama bottoms, grabbed their bags, and pushed out the locker-room doors. Some rinsed off in the large shower stalls in their suits and then undressed under cloak and veil, meaning towel up to collarbone, tucked tight, arm straps pulled down, shirt on, bra on under that. Towel lowered around waist. Suit down around ankles, step out, hold on to towel, step into pants, and presto, magic. All dressed.

Only Cecily Keitel got undressed all the way,

showered like she would in the privacy of her own home. She dried off her back and her arms and even the inside of her thighs and put on her underwear in such a bold and civilized manner that it didn't roll up and catch on her own rear end. Cecily had lived in Europe for the past two years, so nobody blamed her. But nobody wanted to be like her, either.

"Listen, Maggie." Cecily Keitel was one of the last ones in the locker room. She didn't have anyone waiting in the parking lot. She was a junior, and she drove. "You're beginning to piss me off."

Maggie looked around. Her best friend, Julie, had waved and left a few moments ago. The last of the swim team had dried off, more or less, and were gone.

"Who are you trying to impress?" Cecily went on. "Not me, I can tell you that much. Because I know who you are."

At those words, Maggie looked up.

"You think you're better than anyone else. You think you're going to make States your first year on the team."

None of this was true.

Maggie started to speak. "No, I don't," she said.

In a way, she wanted to warn Cecily. She didn't really want to learn what she knew she was about

4

to hear, but it was out of her control. Maggie never knew when it was going to happen, when it wasn't.

"You're a great swimmer. What are you so upset about?" Maggie asked.

"Look, my mother and father got divorced last year," Cecily began. She was hardly putting up a fight at all. "And between the two of them . . . well, it's like . . . they keep fighting over everything: the record collection, the blender, paintings on the walls, the dining-room table, and who gets me."

Maggie listened. She could fill in the emotions because they felt like her own. The tension you feel when your parents are at each other's throats and how it eats at you.

Maggie was still sitting on the narrow locker-room bench, drying her feet. She had her neck bent and was looking up. Cecily was standing, ready to leave but not leaving, as if locked in by the power of true confession.

"Swimming is the only thing I can control," Cecily said. "It's the only thing that belongs to me."

"I can understand that."

Cecily sat down on the bench. "One week after the divorce is final, my dad gets me a new cell phone. The next week my mom buys me an iPad. My dad took me to Bermuda this summer; my mom

5

had to fly us to France for a week. The more they hate each other, the more they pretend to love me."

"I'm sure they love you," Maggie said.

"Maybe," Cecily said, "but they hate each other more. It's really all my mom's fault. She was cheating on him, you know."

Maggie looked away. At the end of each row of lockers was a full-length mirror, reflecting everything within its glass boundaries, no exceptions. Cecily bent over, shaking out her hair with her fingers, and for a second they looked like one body: Maggie's head and torso, Cecily's legs and feet.

"Hey, sorry I said what I said." Cecily straightened up and slipped her swim bag over her shoulder. She was ready to leave.

"What?"

"About you pissing me off. I don't mean it. I'm just a little stressed," Cecily offered, but Maggie knew that within a few minutes, maybe half an hour or more, but definitely sometime after she walked away, Cecily would regret pretty much everything she just said.

It rarely took more than one experience with Maggie to realize that she was not someone you wanted to be around. Hearing yourself tell the truth is uncomfortable, if not downright unpleasant, and Maggie knew, even if no one else understood, that this kind of intimacy made people resent her. It was a gift, and a power, and a burden. It kept her isolated and meant that by the time Maggie got to high school, she was pretty much down to one single friend, Julie Bensimon.

"All you *need* is one friend," her mother would say, covering one of Maggie's schoolbooks in brown paper or setting out dinner and then immediately leaving the room. No one is less inclined to be honest, it would seem, than your own mother.

Maggie's father was a little better at it. Or it was easier for him to maintain the right amount of distance, with pretty much everyone, since Leah drowned. He liked to think of it as discretion. "Discretion," he would say, "is the better part of valor." And Maggie wondered if anyone ever really bought into an expression like that. Wasn't it just a way of granting yourself permission *not* to get involved? An excuse for not being around?

"How was practice, sweetie?" Mr. Paris asked at dinner, which tonight was meat loaf, mashed potatoes, and peas. Each of his bites held a balanced proportion of all three items and just enough condiment. This equation took most of his attention. He didn't look up when he talked.

"Fine," Maggie answered.

"Do you need any money this week?"

"No, Dad."

"Lick hit I," Dylan pronounced, probably meaning something along the lines of the fact that he would like some money this week. He was five, as was, of course, his twin, Lucas.

"Too me," Lucas added. The boys liked to shorten their words, talking backward, sometimes with clicks and odd high-pitched sounds, and they did it quickly. It started when they first began talking, and no one else could understand them. Mr. Paris thought it was just gibberish. Mrs. Paris wanted to have them tested. She feared their strange language had something to do with the in vitro fertilization: some brain malfunction, something serious, something bad. But it turned out only to be twin speak, harmless and common, cute at first, and then annoying, and then distancing.

Leah and Maggie weren't twins. They were almost four years apart and they didn't have a secret language, but they had sister games that they had made up, with rules only they understood and only they could break or change. They played car, with their feet pressed up against each other's, one *driving* while the other provided the engine noises and tire-screeching halts. They had a magazine game: on every page, in every photograph, you had to pick one item you wanted, and you had to pick—even if nothing appealed to you. The challenge was to find something, no matter how small, that you might really want—the watch on the model's hand, a tiny box on the table in the corner of the room behind the piano—because whatever you picked, and touched first on the page, would magically appear in your room the next morning. And the catch was that you were never allowed to explain where any of the stuff came from. It was magic and had to be kept a secret.

Two

"Hey, Maggie. You aren't even listening to me," Julie was saying.

"I am. I am."

Julie kicked her friend under the table. "Then why are you looking over there the whole time? And so what was I just talking about?"

9

Maggie brought her attention back. "You were telling me about the test you have next period on *The Catcher in the Rye* and how you had no idea Holden Caulfield was really supposed to be in a mental hospital at the end and how you are so definitely going to fail. But you're not, Julie. You just say that every time."

Across the cafeteria, three boys stood up. One of them shot his balled-up garbage into a bin; the other two left theirs on the table.

Julie followed her friend's gaze across the cafeteria and figured out what could have possibly captured Maggie's attention more than Holden Caulfield. "Maggie, he's a goon," she said.

"Where do you get a word like that? *Goon.* What's a goon?" Maggie asked. She glanced back at the boys.

"Matthew James is a goon. He's short, he's dumb, and he's captain of the boys' wrestling team. What more do I have to say?"

In truth, Maggie had wondered that herself. If you took Matthew out of the high-school context, there really wouldn't be much, so to speak, other than the fact that he was three years older and had told Maggie he was interested in her. He didn't say *that* exactly, but he did lean over her while she

10

was at his house working on a poster with his younger sister, Jennifer, and say something like "You sure smell good."

And then, instead of "Good-bye," he had said, "See ya," when he was leaving the house.

See ya?

He wanted to see her again.

And he was popular, which still reigned supreme, nearly to the point of suppressing all common sense. Also to his credit, Matthew James had a girlfriend, and she was pretty, and she was cool. She was smart, and kind of an individual, so didn't it stand to reason that if Sarah Lieman liked Matthew, there must be something more to him? Something attractive? Sarah and Matthew could be seen in the halls between classes exchanging all sorts of saliva, with enough passionate groping to have been put on warning by the vice principal. Twice, was the rumor.

Matthew James and his two friends walked out of the cafeteria, kind of swaying, with a sort of gorilla-like gait. He didn't say "See ya" this time, but Maggie figured that was because he hadn't noticed her sitting there.

"Maggie, he has a girlfriend." Julie watched Maggie watching.

"I know. Sarah Lieman."

Maggie and Sarah had actually been in a play together one summer. It was the first summer after Maggie's family moved, five years after Leah drowned, before the twins were born, before Maggie started school, before she met Julie. Sarah was a year older, sixth grade. Her mom directed the community theater playhouse, and Mrs. Paris had put Maggie in the play in order to give her something to do over the summer and as a way to meet kids before school started. Maggie and Sarah got to be natives in the theater's production of *South Pacific,* though once school began in September, they rarely saw each other. The fifth- and sixth-grade wings were on opposite ends of the school, but for those few weeks singing "Bali Ha'i" and painting their faces with dark makeup, Sarah was nice to Maggie, like a big sister, and it did help. She felt less alone.

"C'mon." Julie took Maggie's tray from the table, piled her own leftovers on top, and carried it to the trash. "And tell me why teachers always think we're going to love *The Catcher in the Rye,* because I hated it."

"Teenage rebellion and angst," Maggie answered. "Even though the book is, like, sixty years old, they think we'll relate. Hey, is that where you got the word *goon*?"

"No, that's just a good word." Julie put her arm around Maggie so they could head out into the hall, together. "I like it. And if the shoes fits."

Fifth grade and everything was new. The teachers' names, the hallways, where the bathroom was, all the faces of all the kids, even what to do during recess was all jumbled into a slide show of incomplete and interchangeable pictures. It felt like nearly every minute there was something new to figure out, and an unsettling homesickness followed Maggie around all day. It was October, and substantiating her mother's expression that all you need is one friend, things hadn't gotten better. Maggie sat alone at recess, and today, like yesterday, she watched. She saw one little girl run across the grass, turn, look back, and stumble for a few steps before her knees and palms hit the ground. The rest of her body kind of collapsed in defeat. The girl didn't make any attempt to get up, so Maggie walked over and knelt down on the grass beside her.

"Are you all right?" Maggie asked.

"I fell," the girl said.

The other girls she had been herding with had continued on. If they had noticed her fall, they didn't seem particularly worried. They were all chanting in unison, singing a song Maggie thought she had heard on the car radio. It looked like a hard fall. Now she could see blood seeping through the knee of the girl's pants.

"It hurts," said the girl.

"I'll get someone," Maggie offered, though she really had no idea whom to get or where to go to find someone. There must be a playground monitor, but somehow all the bodies blended together and she could hardly tell who was a kid and who was an adult.

The girl reached out and touched Maggie's arm. "No. Don't. I'm fine. I'm Julie. Are you the new girl?"

Maggie settled down, crossing her legs. "I guess so. I'm Maggie."

"I'm clumsy," Julie said. She winced when she tried to straighten her leg. "My dad wants me to join the swim team. He says it will help me lose a little weight and be better balanced."

By then, several years after Leah's death, Maggie was used to people telling her things they didn't want anyone to know. She also knew that after this

14

girl had told her these personal things, she would never want to talk to Maggie again. She might even spread lies or start rumors to cover up for whatever it was she had revealed.

"You don't need to lose weight. You look fine to me."

Julie smiled. "Thanks."

But maybe this time it wouldn't happen that way. There was something about the way this little girl smiled and cried at the same time, and didn't seem embarrassed by either, that seemed so real.

"Will you be my friend?" Maggie asked her.

"Sure," Julie answered immediately. "Will you be mine?"

Maggie liked Sarah Lieman, respected her, even admired her. But Maggie was obsessed with Matthew, the kind of obsession that is a preoccupation that is like an occupation, so there is no leftover energy to worry about where it came from or where it's going. All brainpower generally allocated to analysis is taken up with the insatiable fueling of that obsession. Lying in bed, before she fell asleep, exhausted by swim practice and whatever homework had kept her up till midnight, Maggie would channel her obsession. She would will her mind to begin dreaming before she entered the stage of rapid eye movement, before she fully lost control of her waking consciousness. She would take control of her dreaming and make it work for her, like a film director, creating a movie in which she was both the scriptwriter and the leading actor.

Like all mind skills, lucid dreaming required practice and hyperconcentration.

And it could only work if the dream was realistic.

The setting and situation had to be familiar and credible. For instance, in her lucid dream, she couldn't run into Matthew on a beach somewhere in the Bahamas, or in some vineyard in Italy, even though that was certainly tempting. Maggie loved the movie *French Kiss* with Meg Ryan and Kevin Kline. Even suspect coincidences were limited. For instance, bumping into Matthew at the mall or on the street outside her house was not allowed. It had to be very close to possible — the more complicated and unpredictable, the more likely to actually occur, the better.

Maggie could feel her body slipping into the fantasy, into lucidity. She feels the roughness of his hands when he grabs her. She can create the pulse of his blood when he holds her. She can feel his breath on her neck when he stands very close to her.

And best of all, in her lucid dream she doesn't have to ask herself or answer to anyone why she is with him, why he is watching her as closely as she watches him. He smells like beer and cigarettes. He talks about nothing but girls and wrestling and monster trucks. He is everything Maggie is not. He is her self-inflicted wound. It is precisely his hollowness and lack of responsibility that draws her to him.

And in her bed, alone at night, it is what draws him to her, until deep, restful sleep finally takes over.

The chance fire drill that brought Maggie and Matthew together probably would have been too contrived for lucid dreaming, but not for real life.

"You're Maggie."

Everyone — teachers, students, administrators — stood somewhere on the grass and behind the faculty parking lot. The signal to return to school hadn't been sounded, and it was long past the normal six minutes, so teachers had given up trying to corral students into lines and keep them quiet. The firefighters and police had already run into the building and were filing out leisurely, so there was clearly no emergency, but no one had yet been allowed back inside.

"You're my little sister's friend, right? I saw you at the house the other day."

"Yeah," Maggie answered.

"You're on the girls' swim team, aren't you?"

"That would be me." Maggie had isolated herself on the grass by the far end of the parking lot. Julie was probably all the way on the other side of the school. She had gym this period, which let out by the main parking lot and the tennis courts.

"It keeps you in nice shape," Matthew said.

His hair was dark, but his eyes were light. He was so close that Maggie could see his eyelashes. And his freckles. The size and shape of his teeth when he spoke. She suddenly became so aware of her own face, every blemish, dot, and asymmetrical arrangement of her features. But he had told her she had a nice shape. What exactly was he looking at? Her waist? Her shoulders? Her ass?

In her lucid sleep state, she would answer coyly.

"If you say so," Maggie said. She licked her lips (they felt dry), untucked her hair from behind her ears (it was uncomfortable), and a second later tucked it back again (it was more uncomfortable).

"So what are you doing this weekend?" Matthew asked her. "What are you doing tonight?"

"Tonight?"

It was Friday and her parents were going out early, taking the twins to dinner and a kiddie show in the city. Maggie had known about it for weeks, and Julie was supposed to come over, but just this morning she had told Maggie that her mom needed her home. *I'm sorry Maggie,* Julie texted during first period. *I can't come over tonight.*

So Maggie would be alone in an empty house.

That was a sign, wasn't it? Like a symbol in a dream?

"I'm home by myself tonight," Maggie told Matthew quickly, too quickly, thinking but not thinking, knowing she was presenting a possibility without really having to decide if she wanted to or not. "My parents are going out."

"So maybe I'll stop by," Matthew told her.

Maggie neglected to mention any of this to Julie after everyone trucked back inside for the remaining half an hour of the school day, during which no one, neither teachers nor students, felt motivated to do any schoolwork. Matthew's maybe-visit seemed to slip Maggie's mind during swim practice as well, and so, by the time evening approached, the window of opportunity to blow the whole thing by her best friend had long since passed.

He probably wouldn't show up anyway, so what was the point?

Three

When she heard wheels pulling over her gravel driveway, an engine cutting off, Maggie darted to the window to look. It was him. He had come. Her parents had been gone for an hour and a half, leaving Maggie nearly the entire time to look at herself in the mirror and imagine what Matthew would see if he looked this closely at her. Or *this* closely. Or *this* closely. She moved back and forth from the glass, trying to approximate average human face-to-face distance, intimate distance, kissing distance even—supposing that was what was going to happen.

She wondered what he would *want* to see and how she might create that for him.

Matthew walked into the house, leaving his friend Dino to wait outside, wait inside a white van (the one with the red and white and green stripes and the logo of shiny tomatoes and fresh parsley) that belonged to Dino's family business. Maggie didn't question why or how long Dino was prepared to wait. Or what he thought was going on inside.

The strong smell of beer preceded Matthew like an announcement and lingered like perfume. Without saying another word after "Hey, are your parents gone?" he pulled Maggie against his body and attached his mouth to hers. Beer. And cheese of some kind? Feta? And somehow it was only a few moments later that they were in Maggie's room, on top of the covers of her bed.

"I really like you, Maggie," Matthew said, lifting his face away from hers.

Well, that was a good thing, wasn't it?

Maggie began to sense that the weight of his body was holding her down. Not that she couldn't have squirmed away or wriggled out (or screamed, for that matter), but then she would appear unhappy, discontent, uncomfortable, and if he got *that* message, he might leave.

"I like you, too," Maggie answered. She let his tongue probe her mouth.

He was directly on top of her, but he wasn't there at all. He was out the door, back in the van, driving away with his friend Dino. He was laughing. He was heading back to Friendly's, where his girlfriend, Sarah, was about to get off from her shift.

Maggie let him force his hand under her clothes, under the waist of her pants, then pull them open—yank off one pants leg but leave the other one on—and somehow during that struggle of zipper and fabric, Matthew had his own jeans down to his ankles. She didn't partake, but she didn't object exactly.

She knew it was what he wanted. She had asked for it, invited him over, expected nothing in return. And she knew it would connect him to her, if only for that brief moment. If her body would only comply with what they were trying to do, then she would have succeeded in a special kind of oblivion.

But it wouldn't.

Matthew rocked and pushed and tried for a while longer, and then his whole body shook and it was over. It wasn't until the white van was gone that Maggie felt her shirt sticking to her stomach and realized what had happened.

Stay inside.

That's all Leah and Maggie had to do, because the condo complex where they lived then was safe.

You needed a code just to drive your car through the electronic gate, and the code was changed every two weeks, all residents informed by e-mail or phone call. And besides, there were kids everywhere, a few older couples, but mostly young families with young children. Everyone knew everyone. If there was a new face along the sidewalk or in the play area, someone was sure to ask who it was, where they were from, what they were doing here. The families got along for the most part, but of course, there was some hierarchy within the development itself.

Condos closer to the entrance, and therefore the highway, were less desirable and cheaper, more often starter homes for young couples before they had kids or had a second kid and moved away. There was more coming and going on that block and less tending to the private landscaping. If a kid lived over by the wall and the highway, they had a harder time breaking in. They might have to be "it" for TV tag or hide-and-go-seek for longer than was fair. Even the maintenance committee seemed part of the conspiracy and repairs for that first row of apartments took longer.

"I'm hot," Maggie whined.

"Well, so? I am too," her older sister told her.

"That's what happens when the air-conditioning breaks."

It was hot, probably hotter, at this point, indoors than out. When their mother left, she made them shut and lock the front door and shut all the first-floor windows. A low ceiling fan turned in slow motion.

"I have an idea."

And now, ten years later, Maggie couldn't remember which one of them actually said that.

"Sorry again about Friday night," Julie was saying. She stood in her bathing suit, her *two* bathing suits—the top one sagging off the other—waiting while Maggie threw her stuff into an empty locker and banged it shut.

"It was fine," Maggie said.

"You could have come to my house, you know."

"I know."

Today Matthew was back with his arm around Sarah, making out with her every few steps they took down the hall.

Wanting something very badly doesn't make it come true, at least not while you are awake. Julie might be sympathetic, if Maggie told her, but it wasn't worth the embarrassment.

"Short course today, remember?" Julie had the bottom of her outer suit, her drag suit, tied into two little bunny ears on each side of her rear end. Only Julie would call attention to that part of her body. She was by far the fullest, roundest girl on the team, and by far the most comfortable with herself.

"Oh, no. I hate short course. I suck at flip turns." Maggie untwisted her shoulder straps and flip-flopped toward the pool entrance.

"You're better than I am," Julie said. "And it doesn't matter; Coach loves you."

"Well, good thing someone does."

"What's that supposed to mean?"

Julie looked like she wanted to say something, ask something. It was her style to bullet Maggie with rapid-fire questions before her friend could close down completely, a verbal blitzkrieg, if you will. But she also knew when it was no use, when prying into whatever secret Maggie was keeping would only drive her further away, and Julie kept quiet.

They both pushed through and out the revolving doors onto the pool deck. Everything was gray—the wet concrete pavement, the massive inflatable cover that extended up twenty-five feet or so, the dim lights—but mostly the water, murky, fifty meters long, ten lanes across, bobbing with lane markers, waiting.

Coach Mac began shouting commands as soon as all the girls were present. The fastest swimmers — he pointed — were assigned lanes 1 and 2, and so on down the line. Six girls per lane. The warm-up was scribbled on the whiteboard in purple marker. One by one the girls had to stop talking to one another and line up. The chatter echoing across the pool diminished in increments. The assistant coach blew the whistle five seconds apart, followed by the sound of someone plunging into the water, until it was quiet but for the rhythmic splashes, the flutter-kicking, and the steady roar of the warm air being blown into the dome, holding it all up.

As soon as she was underwater, Maggie heard the quiet, though every sound was amplified in her ears and in her brain, the speed rushing past, the impact of her own hand, the sucking in of air and water, mixed, the faraway sound of her feet breaking the surface. She was aware of the glide and of the pull, the power of her body working, arms and legs and head, mouth open, elbow bent. Pull and glide. Pull and glide. Sound, like shame, travels four times faster under the water.

Maggie's mother heard the sirens before she pulled up, and out her car window she saw all the people gathered around the pool. Her first thought was thank goodness the sound wasn't coming from her block, from her condo, overlooking the highway, where her two daughters were inside waiting for her.

Whatever is happening, it's none of my business. I need to get back to the house, to the girls. Unload these groceries and start some lunch.

Mrs. Paris turned her head away from the fencing, the pool, and started to turn the car around the next corner, heading home. And then something made her look again toward the noise, toward the chaos, the clamor of people, the energy of panic that seeped right in through her closed windows and blast of air-conditioning. She hated herself for looking, for being silently satisfied that the tragedy was someone else's and not her own.

The crowd was gathering around a little body that lay on the grass, the body of a girl in a green-and-yellow bathing suit. Mrs. Paris saw the ambulance and the EMS people working at a frantic, desperate pace. She drew in one last breath of relief, knowing that her two little girls, Maggie and Leah, were back in the house safe. If she could rewind time and live again in the moment before her heart allowed her mind to recognize the long, wet brown hair, the long skinny legs, she would, of course — she did — again and again and again.

Third period, Algebra I, was the only class Julie and Maggie had together. As she did in every class, Maggie took the seat closest to the back of the room. Julie had tried to sit next to her, but about a week into September, Mrs. Michelangelo caught on and moved them apart.

"Something happened, Mags. You don't even have to tell me. I know something's wrong."

Mrs. Michelangelo had left the room. No one really wondered why; it was more like the effect of a sudden wind on dried leaves. All at once, everyone started moving, and a few kids left altogether. Now Julie was sitting on top of Maggie's desk. Maggie stayed in her seat. They created a small universe of two.

"Nothing," Maggie said.

"It's a boy, isn't it?"

"No."

"I know it is. And I bet I know who," Julie went on. "It's that shithead Matthew James and you're major crushing on him."

"He's not that bad."

"Seriously?"

But Maggie didn't have time to respond. Mrs. Michelangelo still hadn't returned. Mr. Goss, the vice principal, entered instead.

"There's fifteen more minutes of class," he said. "I trust you can all find something productive to do."

He sat down at the teacher's desk and offered no further explanation about Mrs. Michelangelo's disappearance. He looked stoically out at the class, like a captain in rough seas.

The boy in front of Maggie turned around in his chair. "I bet I know what happened."

He had the local area code shaved into the very short hair on the side of his head and a diamond earring, too big to be real. Maggie remembered he was in her seventh-grade English, but other than that she didn't know much about him, except his name, Tommy. Maggie tried to give Julie that please-don't-encourage-him look, but it was too late.

"Yeah, how's that?" Julie asked. She had slid off the desk and into the seat next to Maggie.

"My mother and Mrs. Michelangelo went to college together. Or high school—I don't remember."

Which seemed kind of interesting, so Maggie said, "Really?"

"You think I'd make that up?" Tommy snapped back.

"No, I mean, *Really*. Like, *Really, that's pretty cool*," Maggie said.

"Oh, yeah, it is," Tommy continued. "So, they're friends, and I happen to know that Mrs. Michelangelo's husband is in big trouble. He's going to lose his business and maybe their house."

"So what does that have to do with Mrs. Michelangelo leaving the room?" Julie asked.

"It just probably does. They owe tons of taxes and they can't pay their mortgage. Which is funny, since my family doesn't even have our own house."

The girls exchanged looks. Maggie had often shared the strange confessional experiences she had with Julie.

"We rent above Smitty's Garage, you know. My dad does leaves and mows lawns. He probably mows your lawn."

"My dad cuts his own grass," Julie said.

"Yeah, well," Tommy said. "He's the only one in town, then."

Over the years, Maggie noticed that truths came in categories. Mostly they were things someone was embarrassed about, a physical thing or an emotional issue, or a social problem, real or imagined.

Home life, personal life. The only common denominator was that everyone seemed to think everyone *else* had it all together.

"It really sucks being the poorest kid in town," Tommy said. "It's all bullshit. Dirt is dirt, especially if you move it to make a living. I die every time my dad comes to one of my soccer games and I am sure he has spread fertilizer for one of the other dads sitting there. Sometimes I pretend I don't see him."

"See who?" Julie asked.

"My dad."

Judging from the way he was beginning to tear up, Maggie knew there was more.

"But last year was the worst, when my dad wanted to coach the JV baseball team. He played, you know. My dad. He had one season in the majors. He's really good. He's a great dad. He taught me how to throw, catch grounders, stay in front of the ball. He taught me everything, never put me down, always encouraged me. He wouldn't even have cared if I sucked at baseball. He just wanted to coach. And I lied to him."

Now Tommy's voice took on a shaky, higher pitch and a couple of other students were turning around to see what was going on. Lucky for him, more than half the class had left.

"I came home and told him not to bother apply-ing 'cause they already had someone in mind. 'But I was in the pros,' he told me. 'Who could they have possibly gotten?'

" 'I guess they got someone better,' I said. I didn't know what else to say. And my dad never bothered to call the athletic office and find out if it was true. He just took my word for it."

Maggie could feel the burn behind her eyes, but she blinked it away. Everyone, it seems, wants abso-lution for something.

Four

Matthew came over to see Maggie precisely two more times that school year. During the first of those two evenings, he tried again to make him-self one with the girl who seemed accommodating, if not entirely willing. No one was waiting in the driveway outside, and this time they didn't make it to the bedroom. Matthew kissed her hard, hold-ing her up against the kitchen wall after accepting Maggie's offer of a drink of water. He put down his glass and pulled Maggie to the floor with him. He landed with a thud, and she, only slightly more gracefully, on top of him.

Again, there didn't seem to be time to wonder if this was what she wanted—whether it was wise or safe. Maggie tried to ignore the sharp pain in her back as the bones of her spine were pressed against the tile-hard floor, her underpants pulled to the side, bunched up and wedged uncomfortably into her bottom. Once again, it didn't work, but once again, Matthew seemed to achieve some kind of success even if she had failed again.

The second time was two months later, when Maggie's parents and brothers went out for the afternoon. He made his feeble attempts to enter but quickly resorted to rubbing himself up against Maggie's bare thigh without bothering to take off his pants.

By June, Matthew had left town, working in Myrtle Beach, South Carolina, for the summer, and then heading off for his freshman year of college at SUNY Albany.

Five

Maggie's sophomore year of high school began with two lofty goals—one public, one private.

To help the girls' varsity swim team make it to States. To have sex, sexual intercourse, by the time Matthew James returned home for Thanksgiving break.

She would, then, surprise him on his next attempt with not only her willingness and accommodation, but with her skill. Basically her hymen, her cherry, her maidenhead, her virginity, would be broken, and everything could move smoothly forward for Matthew.

But this second goal, of course, was not something she talked about. Not even to Julie.

"I hate start drills," Julie whispered to Maggie. Swim practice start drills meant that there were no assigned lanes; no matter the hierarchy of your finish times, all the girls lined up behind whichever blocks they wanted.

"I know. I got your back."

Both girls watched a senior swimmer, Maxine Eldon, take her place on the starting block in their line. The girl next in line got ready to whip around the Styrofoam noodle and whack her in the legs before Maxine had a chance to dive forward.

"On your marks," Coach Mac shouted. He put the whistle up to his mouth and held it between his teeth.

Maxine stretched out and gripped the base of the rubber starting block. A false start, even, or especially, with the threat of being hit with the wet noodle, meant coming back and doing it again.

"Get set."

She bent her knees and froze into position.

But there was no punishment for hitting someone before the whistle. It was, in fact, a cheap chance to hit somebody as hard as you possibly could.

There was a split second while Maxine seemed suspended in air, leaning her weight as far out across the pool as she could without letting go, trusting the third call would follow. Coach Mac blew his whistle. There was a thunderous lunge forward, eight Styrofoam noodles landed their marks, and the swimmers hit the water.

"Is this really supposed to make us better starters?" Julie leaned toward her friend. She was next in line to do the hitting.

"C'mon," the girl in front said, turning around. "Really give it to me this time. You're such a wuss, Julie. C'mon. I can take it."

The problem was, you had to swing the noodle fast and hard, otherwise it didn't land. It just kind of flopped and missed.

"I'm not a wuss. I just don't like hitting people," Julie said.

"I'm going to hit you, Julie," Maggie said, "as soon as you pass me that noodle. So you might as well get yours in."

The girl stepped up on the starting block. She turned back and smiled. "Not too hard, though. OK?"

Her name was Rebecca, another sophomore, and so at one time or another she had probably told Maggie something she wished she hadn't. It might have been a couple of years ago, or maybe it was just last year. Maybe about eating too much, or not eating, or about her unnatural fear of stairwells— maybe Rebecca had forgotten the whole thing by now. As she dove into the water and Julie halfheartedly smacked her with the purple noodle, Maggie remembered what it was. Rebecca hadn't gotten her period yet, and her parents were taking her to an endocrinologist. Big deal.

The coach worked them hard that afternoon, particularly hard, and Maggie particularly harder. He had a lot of expectations for her. He wanted the team to qualify for the state championship.

"Head down." He paced alongside her lane shouting out adjustments and calling out her split times. Maggie could hear his muffled voice as her head turned back and forth in the water, like a radio station tuning in and tuning out. Maggie swam, allowing the ache in her shoulders, and hips, and ankles, and back, and lungs to fill her with strength. It was, as Cecily Keitel had said, something she could control. Underneath the water, she found air.

Condos that faced the pool, of course, were the most expensive, and those kids acted like they were better than everyone else. Leah had a friend who lived in one of those, though "friend" was a loose term. It seemed to Maggie that her older sister didn't really like Meghan Liggett, or Meghan Liggett didn't much like Leah. It was just a feeling she got from watching them together, at the pool and on the school bus. But Leah had never said that. She called Meghan her friend, and she would bark at her sister if Maggie tried to point out anything to the contrary.

Lately, the past few days, if Maggie thought about it, her sister seemed more annoyed at her. As if the difference between being nine and being five had gotten deeper. The space between them changing as unpredictably as Leah's moods themselves. Sometimes she wanted Maggie to play with her; sometimes she didn't. Sometimes she liked her little sister; other times she shouted at her and told her to leave her alone. So a little sister needs to learn how to work the system, even if she doesn't quite understand it herself.

"I have an idea."

It *was* Maggie.

"Let's go see if Meghan's home. I bet her house isn't so hot as this."

"Mom told us to stay here." But Leah was considering it; Maggie could tell. She liked that, and it made Maggie feel important. Maybe this would be one of those times Leah wanted to play with Maggie.

"I won't tell," Maggie said.

"You always tell on me. And I always get in trouble."

That wasn't true, but Maggie could see how it looked that way. If there was a fight, or even raised voices, if her parents heard but didn't see something

38

get knocked over, if the fridge was left open or there were crumbs on the counter, they always blamed Leah first. They acted as if they were concerned only with ending the fight, quieting the voices, or preventing further damage, but, when in doubt, their parents usually took Maggie's side, because it was easier.

"I promise I won't. We could even go for a swim and cool off."

Maggie waited in the shower after swim practice until she heard everyone leave. It took a while. Julie was, of course, the hardest to get rid of.

"I'm fine," Maggie called out from behind the industrial white plastic. "I want to condition my hair. I might even take a sauna."

Because of the fact that no one *ever* went in the sauna, other than the time in middle school that they had a swim meet in Montreal, Canada, Julie wasn't buying it. Those girls in Canada took off all their clothes while getting dressed. They rubbed down their glistening wet legs and arms with their towels while standing completely naked beside their lockers. They even talked to one another while dousing themselves with body lotion and powder. One of the Canadian swimmers, the one who had won in backstroke, actually stood completely nude, her towel lying on the bench in a crumpled heap, while she rolled deodorant under her arms. They made Cecily Keitel look like a prude.

There was no way Maggie was taking a sauna.

"I'll wait," Julie called back into the shower curtain.

"No, go, Julie. I'm fine. I'm taking the late bus. It's always late—you know that. I'll call you when I get home."

"If you want to be alone, Mags," Julie said finally, "just say so. I know you, and I still love you."

"I'm sorry."

"No need," Julie called out. She grabbed her stuff, waved back toward the showers, and left.

Slowly the locker room sounds diminished: the last toilet flushed; the few remaining voices drifted toward the hall. You weren't supposed to have cell phones near the pool, but the girls turned them on as soon as they got out of the water. Eventually, even the musical rings and beeps of voice messages and chimes of texts stopped. Maggie wrung out her bathing suit, rolled it up, wrapped a second towel around her waist, and stepped out into the locker room. Other than the steady drips of wet bathing suits secured by their straps to the outside of the lockers, it was quiet.

As she passed one of the long mirrors at the end of the aisle, Maggie paused. She stood facing herself and then slowly let her towel drop completely to the floor. She was naked, full frontal, so unfamiliar — like a drawing from her health book, the one that showed the stages of puberty. How could her own image be so foreign to her?

Well, in her own defense, she hadn't had much opportunity to stare at herself nude. At home there was always worry of her brothers barging in or banging on the bathroom door. Besides, the only full-length mirror was in her parents' bedroom. Who stands naked in their parents' room?

Maggie could feel goose bumps rise up so suddenly on her skin they hurt. She had read once that a mirror image is not a true representation of one's self. It is a *reverse* image, and if you could ever really see yourself the way others see you — because still photography or even a video is a flat and altered one-dimensional image — you wouldn't recognize yourself.

Yet, here she was, her flesh dripping with water, tight with cold. The curve of her hips, the darkness

41

between her legs. Her shoulders, broad from swimming. Her neck, her chin, her lips. The long bones of her shins stuck out. The tendons of her feet and toes were flexed and visible. Her wet hair stuck to her neck and down her back, here and there, clumped together. Her belly, both flat and soft, inviting as a woman's. Here was her body, stretching and pulling and yearning in ways that Leah's never had.

Here was Maggie, seven years older than her sister would ever get to be.

Her brothers clamored around Maggie when she came home from practice.

"Daddy's home not tonight. Eat we get in front of the TV," Dylan sang.

When Mr. Paris was on a business trip, not only did they scrap the family dinner, but usually the boys slept in bed with their mother.

"Oh, right." Maggie stopped. She dropped her swim bag on the floor. "So what's for dinner?"

Lucas answered. The boys would talk like that, taking turns in an easy synchronization. "Spaghetti and."

"Meat sauce," Dylan finished.

"Sounds good." Maggie left her swim bag on the

floor and hoisted her knapsack higher on her shoulder. "I gotta start my homework. Where's Mom?"

"In the."

"Kitchen," Lucas said.

Maggie poked her head in, leaving her body outside, her hands holding on to the door frame.

"Hi, Mom. I'm home."

"Oh, you are."

Her mother looked up with surprise from the counter, where she was cutting carrots, but of course, she had heard the door open. She probably heard the boys talking and Maggie's voice. She would have heard the flop of the swim bag, heavier footsteps. The thing was, Mrs. Paris never missed a beat. Mr. Paris called it Paranoid Hearing.

A mother's hearing, Mrs. Paris would snap back.

But Maggie could remember when Mrs. Paris would drop everything to be waiting by the front door when Leah's school bus hissed to a stop in front of the house. As soon as Leah walked into the house, Mrs. Paris would offer her something to eat and then ask a million questions while she nibbled on Goldfish or cut-up apples.

How was your day? How was the bus ride? Did you get your spelling test back yet? Didn't you have gym today?

And Maggie would sit at the counter dreaming about the day that she and her big sister would get off the bus together and she would come home to yummy snacks and someone rifling through her knapsack, asking questions.

"How was practice?" Mrs. Paris went back to her carrots but didn't expect or wait for an answer. "We'll be eating in about half an hour, OK?" And that was it.

"Sure, Mom. I'll be in my room."

For a while, Maggie focused on algebra and her history paper on the Second Congo War, until the urge to check her Facebook grew too strong. She went on Matthew's page, clicking on his friends, studying the photos, referencing and cross-referencing. She would go back to reading about Zaire, but Maggie's mind kept returning irrationally to Matthew, over and over. Like the pull of the moon on the tides of the ocean.

So Maggie picked Nathan.

She picked him because he looked nice, and from what Maggie could tell, he *was* nice. He was a junior, a year older than she was. He wasn't on the wrestling or football team; he wasn't popular, but he wasn't *un*popular. He had dark, wavy hair and was tall and thin, borderline skinny—nothing like Matthew James. He didn't have a girlfriend. He worked after school. He didn't look like the big drinking type, though who could really tell?

And the first thing Maggie decided to do was to leave a flower on Nathan's car as a kind of subliminal message (another reason she picked him—Nathan had a car, which seemed integral to her plan). If all went well, by Thanksgiving break Maggie would no longer be a virgin. Matthew would reap the benefits, and beyond that she hadn't really thought it out all that well.

"Why are you buying flowers?" Julie asked. "I thought you didn't like strong perfumey smells. Lilies smell like crazy, you know."

"Just one," Maggie said. The drama club had a table set up in the hall for their annual Blossoms for Off-Off-Broadway fund-raiser. Cari Stone was manning the table. "It's for a good cause."

Julie looked skeptical, but Cari nodded enthusiastically.

"It is," Cari said. "We're doing *Twelve Angry Men* this fall. Only we don't have enough boys trying out, so we're changing it to *Twelve Angry Jurors,* but it's going to be great."

Cari was always enthusiastic. It was her most annoying quality.

Last year in the girls' bathroom, and in the time it took to stand side by side at the communal sink washing their hands, Cari had told Maggie her life's story.

"I'm an actor, and actors have nothing to hide. That's what being a good actor is all about," Cari said, and then proceeded to explain to Maggie why she didn't want anyone to know that her grand-mother was such-and-such famous movie direc-tor, because then everyone would think that's why she got the best parts in the school plays. Maggie wanted to tell Cari that everybody already knew that and that it probably *was* why she got all the best parts, but it didn't seem to matter.

Because now all Maggie wanted was to buy a flower. It was step one of her plan.

"That's five dollars, please."

"For one flower?" Julie asked.

"Well, it *is* a fund-raiser."

Maggie reached into her coat pocket and took out a ten-dollar bill. "Want one?" she asked Julie.

"Sure," Julie answered.

Six

Nathan never got the flower—not that he would have known what it meant if he had (subliminal message notwithstanding)—because Maggie put it on the wrong car. She snuck out to the parking lot during lunch and slipped it under the windshield wiper of a dark-blue, four-door Volvo with a banged-up bumper and a missing passenger-side door handle, but apparently there were two of those at the high school.

But it was a bad plan anyway. She didn't leave a note, which turned out to be a very good thing, since the other blue, beat-up Volvo sedan belonged to the health teacher, Mr. Edgerton, and he might not have understood. Anyway, even if Maggie had found the right car, she wouldn't have known what to write.

Hello there. I have been trying to lose my virginity and I picked you to do it with. Wondering what you're doing later on this afternoon?

In hindsight, Maggie realized she hadn't worked out the kinks in her plan. It might be better to try to be in the *right place at the right time*—an accidentally-on-purpose kind of thing. It wasn't such a big school. Not even that big of a town. One market. One post office, liquor shop, pharmacy, hardware store, dry cleaner. Friendly's Ice Cream, of course. It would be a matter of making the most of the right time when it materialized. It was early October. She had to be patient.

There was a text message on Maggie's phone when she got out of swim practice the next afternoon. It was from her dad telling her that he was going to be about ten (which meant twenty-five) minutes late, and Maggie decided to start walking toward town rather than wait. She figured her dad would see her on the road and stop. Worst-case scenario, he would get to the high school and call her cell when he didn't see her standing outside the entrance to the pool. The other girls were filing out of the gym, to their cars or waiting parents, or friends. Maggie assured Julie that her dad was on his way, and she started walking. Maggie made it about ten yards down the road.

Nathan was just standing there, on the side of the road, facing her.

It was so odd, and so unlikely, that for a long second Maggie wondered if he had been waiting. If somehow he had gotten wind of her plan and had come to call her out — or take her up on it, as the case may be. For that one prolonged second, she felt caught, and her heart beat nervously. Why was he standing here on the road like that? No one walks to town from the high school. No one even walks on this road.

What am I, crazy?

"My car won't start," Nathan offered.

"Huh?"

"That's why I'm walking to town."

"Oh."

"I heard you walking behind me, so I stopped and waited."

"Oh."

"I mean, it would seem silly to just keep walking, right? If we're both going the same way."

"I guess."

"Actually, I think I'm just out of gas."

It was going to take a few more seconds to figure it all out.

"You're Maggie, aren't you? Paris? I thought I heard someone behind me. People don't usually walk on School Road, so I turned around and looked. Hope I didn't startle you. You look startled. You OK?"

"Oh, yeah. I'm fine. Sorry," Maggie answered.

He sounded sweet, because, Maggie thought, that word really does mean something. *Sweet.* And up close, he was beautiful. Up close, he was better looking than from across the parking lot or cafeteria, from where she had done most of her reconnaissance. He had blue eyes and half-moon lids, and he seemed really nice.

Sweet.

By the time they had walked less than half the distance to town, Nathan had already told her about his family, his mom and dad, his sisters and brothers. There were five of them in total, five Carpenter children. He asked Maggie about swim team and their next meet, which was tomorrow. He listened when she answered. She found herself telling him about Lucas and Dylan, their funny secret language, and though usually she decided to leave out the part about *once* having had an older sister, Maggie found this time to be different.

"My sister, Leah, died when I was five."

Nathan didn't say what everyone always said, something like, "Geez, I'm so sorry." Or: "Oh, my best friend's cousin had a friend who died." Or: "That almost happened to me once." Which is why Maggie had long since decided it was easier to just omit that part of her history.

So when her father finally pulled up to the side

of the road and looked once at Nathan but said nothing more than hello, Maggie felt she had chosen wisely.

No one came to a swim meet unless they had to. Swim meets were probably the most boring sporting events in all high-school history. There was a lot of waiting: so many heats in each race, so many swimmers in each heat. Meets were interminable, and even if you were rooting for someone, once the actual swimmers were in the water, they all looked the same. And swim meets were unrelentingly loud. Sounds echoed off the walls and thudded on the surface of the water. The constant splashing, whistle blowing, and cheering took on a kind of canned, unreal quality.

Maggie hated the actual meets. She usually found herself hiding in the bathroom with cramps just before her race was announced, and because of this, Maggie had sussed out the least-used bathrooms in all the local schools and health clubs, even if it meant using an empty boys' locker room after school hours.

"Hey, you swim the fifteen hundred free, don't you?"

Maggie turned from the sink to the sound of a girl's voice. It was a girl from the other team, Franklin High School. Maggie recognized her from last year and years before that. They swam a lot of the same events.

"You must be as nervous as me."

"Probably more," Maggie said. She cranked the handle on the dispenser to dry her hands, but the paper towels were stuck or missing.

"We both better get out of the boys' locker room. The wrestling team comes in for late practices Thursday afternoons."

"Thanks for telling me." Maggie pulled open the heavy door, and both girls stepped out. The boys' locker room was at the other end of the school from the pool, but the faraway sounds of the meet and the faint smell of chlorine were wafting down the hall.

"I hate swim meets," the girl said.

"Me too. I'm Maggie."

"I know who you are. I'm Kiah." She smiled. "I mean, you always win, so I know your name. That's probably why you don't know me."

Maggie wanted to say something nice to counter that, but it was true, and she couldn't think of anything.

"Don't worry about it. I don't care," Kiah said after a long silence. "I just don't want to go back in there yet. Do you?"

"Not really."

The girls pressed their backs to the wall, bent their knees, and let their bottoms sink to the floor.

"I should probably watch my best friend's race, though. She always cheers *me* on." Maggie meant Julie. Julie swam the early heats. She wasn't expected to place, but you never knew.

"You have a best friend?" Kiah began. "I have a best friend. Or at least I used to."

Sometimes Maggie had a warning, and sometimes she could even look back and see how she had affected the whole thing, maybe by asking leading questions or seeming overly interested, but sometimes these intimate confessions came out of nowhere, out of the blue. There was nothing Maggie could pinpoint as evoking such intimacy with an acquaintance, someone she knew vaguely or just met. It was almost as if the less connected she was, the closer she could become.

"My best friend hates me," Kiah went on. "We just had this huge fight. She says I talk about her behind her back."

Maggie didn't ask for further clarification, but

she nodded, and that was all Kiah seemed to need. "I don't say anything I wouldn't say right to her face, you know. Some people just can't stand hearing the truth about themselves. Like, I told her she shouldn't go out with that guy from West Hill—people will think she's a slut. I didn't say she *was* a slut."

Maggie stood up. "I better go. Good luck with your friend."

"Yeah, thanks. You too. Nice talking to you."

Just like that, people told her things, drank her in, a wellspring in the wilderness.

Maggie hadn't expected to see Nathan at the meet. She had no way of knowing how long he had been there.

That was him, wasn't it?

It was. There he was, sitting at the very top, on the highest bench of the bleachers, his back leaning against one of the metal poles. Everyone was gathering their bags, their towels, slipping on pajama bottoms and sweatshirts. Parents milled around while coaches confirmed times and future competitions.

When he thought he had caught her eye, Nathan waved. Maggie tried to remember if he had told her he had a sister on the team, or on the other team. Why else would he be here? He must have come to see her. Maggie lifted her hand and waved back, just enough to show interest but not enough to seem too interested. After all, this was *her* plan, and it needed to go accordingly.

Maggie couldn't swim, but Leah could, of course. Leah had passed the deep-water test at Camp Jekocee, though maybe that was because the camp lifeguard was flirting with the girls' third-grade counselor when Leah had held on to the side of the pool on her way back.

But the morning the two sisters sat in their bathing suits, green-and-yellow daisies and sun-bleached bunches of red berries, by the stairs at the shallow end of their condo pool and cooled their feet, no one was thinking about that.

"So isn't this good?" Maggie said. She splashed the water.

"Yeah, this is good," Leah agreed. She let her eyes wander to the front windows of condos A–C, the ones that looked out onto the pool, the one where Meghan lived. "We gotta go back soon, though."

"I'm gonna swim, then," Maggie said. She stood up and took two steps into the water.

"Oh, no, you're not." Leah turned back to look at her sister.

Suddenly this little adventure struck Leah as very wrong. Leah was the responsible one. She was the older sister. She was supposed to be watching Maggie. All they had to do was stay in the house. Her mother would be mad, so mad. She would see the wet bathing suits. She would see footprints on their front step. Maybe she would come home early.

No, Leah hadn't thought this through at all. They needed to get back to the house before their mother did. Air-conditioning or not.

"What?" Maggie twisted her hips around. The water was already up to her knees. Her feet looked funny, distorted, like they weren't attached to her body, dissolving in the sunlight that reflected off the surface.

"You can't go in," Leah said.

Can't? There were so many things Leah could do that Maggie wasn't allowed to, so many more things Leah *told* her she couldn't do. Leah got to stay up later. She got to say no when she didn't want to eat something. Maggie always had to *try it first.* Leah got to sit in the front seat when there were only three of them. She got to order a whole meal in a restaurant, and half the time Leah didn't finish hers, either.

"You can't swim," Leah told her little sister. "You don't know how."

"So?" Maggie shot back. "Neither do you."

Seven

It was a rare time when Dylan and Lucas weren't together, but today Dylan was alone in Maggie's room. Lucas had gone to the dentist to have a cavity filled, but only after being convinced that Dylan *didn't* have one but that Lucas *did*. That's why he had to go and his brother didn't. They were still adjusting to not being in the same class for kindergarten. As Mrs. Paris predicted, it had made them cling more to each other, not less, as the school psychologist had insisted.

Though now, without his slightly larger and three-second-older brother, Dylan was more talkative. He had already gone through everything in Maggie's room, touching, looking, asking questions.

"Can I have this, Mags?" Dylan was on Maggie's bed, on his back, holding up a small pedometer. It had belonged to Leah.

"Where did you get that?"

"In that drawer, Maggie. Was it Leah's?"

Dylan and Lucas weren't afraid to ask for anything they wanted or needed, nor were they afraid to talk about Leah. They had no memory of her, no guilt, no sadness. She was four letters, L-E-A-H, from the alphabet they copied into homework notebooks, and nothing more than that. Like a photograph of your great-uncle who was killed before you were born, in a war that you've only vaguely even heard of.

"'No' and 'Yes,' Dylan. Sorry," Maggie told him. She had her feet propped up on her desk, her laptop on her knees, but she leaned forward and snatched the pedometer out of his hands. Sometimes it felt like the twins were from a different set of parents, but of course they weren't. They were just from a different marriage, a different life.

Leah had begged for that pedometer. She made her case (as was Leah's unrelenting style) that she would use it all the time, and how educational it was, and how she would take really good care of it. It wasn't that expensive, she pointed out. Her mom thought it was a strange request for a nine-year-old, and her dad didn't want to indulge Leah's need to buy everything she saw on TV commercials. But in the end, she got it for her birthday. She used it twice and put it away in a drawer, and now it was Maggie's.

"C'mon, Magmag. It's so cool, and you never use it." Funny how he spoke perfectly well when he wanted something. "Why can't I have it?"

Maggie flung the pedometer onto the end of her bed and turned around in her chair again. She was about to answer, to tell her brother why he couldn't have anything of Leah's that belonged to her. The front door opened; their mom was home from the dentist, and it sounded like Mr. Paris had come home at the same time. They walked into the house shouting at each other, in that muffled, stilted way they somehow believed was quiet. Did they really think that no one could hear every word they were saying? Maggie tried to remember a time when their piercing, angry tone was rare, when it would have startled or surprised her, but she couldn't. Was it before Leah? Or just after?

When her mother first told her about the impending twins, Maggie clearly remembers wondering why her parents were having more children. Aren't you supposed to love each other when you have babies?

Her parents' voices made their way up the stairs.

What do you think? I'm home all day taking tennis lessons?

Well, it would be nice if you picked up the laundry once in a while.

This was unexpected. I needed to get Lucas to the dentist. The dry cleaner's is on the other end of town.

The door slammed.

Maggie watched as Dylan's entire face changed. His eyes dimmed; his mouth tightened. His whole presence looked smaller. She could see it in his eyes, and she could feel it in her own body. No matter how used to it she was, it made her sick.

Lucas's footsteps banged up the stairs. Dylan hopped off Maggie's bed to meet him in the hall, and they disappeared into their room. When Maggie looked over at her bed for the pedometer, she saw that it was gone, too.

"So who is this Nathan?" Julie asked. She took a bite of her sandwich and then set it down. "God, I hate peanut butter and honey."

"I thought you liked it," Maggie said. "Banana?"

"Don't change the subject."

"I didn't change it—you did."

There was a pause in the cafeteria noise. Maggie had once read that there is a natural lull in all conversations, every seven minutes. And then someone notices it, or everyone notices, feels really uncomfortable, and picks it up again. Silence is not well tolerated, like lying. As if on cue, the noise level rose again in a wave.

"So who is he?" Julie asked again.

Maggie lowered her voice. "He's some boy. You know him. He's a year ahead of us."

"Oh, c'mon, Maggie. I mean, who *is* he?"

Instead of answering, Maggie looked around the room. Stacy Ketchum was, once again, throwing her uneaten lunch in the trash. Brendon Fox was flicking Poland Spring bottle tops across the room. Cari Stone was running lines from *Twelve Angry Jurors* with Zoe Lowenbein, who had recently taken Lowen as a stage name, on the advice of her New York City talent agent. Josh Jamner, Daniel Wu, and Cody Shea were in a heated discussion about last night's play-off game. In the corner by the window, two boys Maggie didn't know were playing chess, as they did every afternoon. Everything was just as it always was.

"It's a good thing I don't have whatever it is you always say you have," Julie said, not so quietly. She pushed the rest of her lunch across the table.

"What?" Maggie tried to sound like she didn't know what Julie meant.

"You know, whatever it is you think you have that makes people tell you about themselves— well, it's just very convenient that it doesn't seem to work on you. Because then," she went on, "you'd be telling me the truth, instead of this bullshit about *some boy.*"

Maggie reached her hand out, palm up. A peace offering. "I am, Jules. I don't know. Right now he's just some boy that I kinda like."

Julie's voice lowered. "OK, so say I believe you. What's going on with him? You really *like* him, like him?"

"Yeah, I guess so," Maggie said.

"Well, anyone or anything that gets you to forget about that douche bag Matthew James is OK with me."

Maggie said quickly, "Nathan is going to drive me home from the PSATs tomorrow."

"Then you don't need a ride from me. Okeydokey." She smiled at her friend. "Sounds like you have a plan." Julie winked.

The plan:

Maggie had dug out her eighth-grade health notebook, flipping through the pages until she found the section "Sex Education," which at the time she had paid no attention to, just diligently copied the SMART Board notes into her notebook. The instructor was Mr. Cilberto, shy and quiet, and the assistant wrestling coach, by coincidence. He didn't talk much about the list of birth control methods as he wrote in tiny letters on the board. It all seemed to embarrass him terribly, but he put ABSTINENCE on the top in big letters, followed by the others.

The rhythm method was number three.

The timing was just right, seven days from the end of her last menstrual cycle. Safe for intercourse and prevention of pregnancy. It wasn't advisable necessarily, but it was a viable plan and one Maggie planned on using.

The girls were dressing for practice, yanking on their suits, or two, one over the other for extra resistance, tying up their hair, stepping into flip-flops. That afternoon, there was to be a mandatory film on water safety before practice. No one was excused, not even seniors, who had heard the Red Cross spiel three times before. Though somehow Maggie had managed to be absent last year.

"No one can skip this," Coach Mac told them.

The whole team squeezed into the coach's office, sitting mostly cross-legged on the floor, a couple on top of the desk and the filing cabinet. These girls were used to being close together, breathing to the sound of one another's breath. Often they swam with only a foot or two between bodies, in full stride. A touch of someone's toes during a flip turn to signal the need to cut ahead, all in a smooth rhythm, like a machine, and now they sat, bored and restless, packed tightly, fish out of water.

"Lights out," Coach Mac called. The girl nearest the wall switch stood up; everything went dark, and a low whispering began immediately. The video suffused the room in a hazy light.

"Quiet down, everyone."

A white-sand beach. The peaceful dark-blue ocean. Jump-cut to an aqua-blue pool, the painted black line wavering under the water. All stillness, all calm. A family on a boat. A couple picnicking by a lake. There were comments here and there from the girls, giggles and jokes. Maggie sat leaning her back against the doorjamb, Julie next to her.

A child wanders off. The young woman in the couple decides to swim by herself. The family in the boat encounters some bad weather. And in each case someone nearly drowns.

Water is wet. The sun hot. The concrete burning. The sirens loud. The voices frantic. The water is covering her head. There are no words, no directions.

No sound at all. One man is waving his arms like a lunatic, grabbing the head of the person trying to save him, dragging them both under.

There is an image. A narrative. Actors. Water.

People on the shore making a chain with their hands, a woman in a boat throwing out a rope, a life preserver, a plastic blow-up chair. A lifeguard in red runs across the beach.

Reach. Throw. Go. The words flash across the screen.

On the grass, in the boat, on the beach, the people so brave and so determined. The body is not moving; the arms are limp. Tipping back the head, checking the mouth. Then pressing and blowing and working so hard for someone they don't even know.

"I knew this was a bad idea." Julie reached over and touched Maggie's shoulder. "Are you OK?"

"Yeah," Maggie answered.

"No, you're not. C'mon, let's get outta here."

When Mr. and Mrs. Paris moved out of the condo, they hoped that only good memories would come with them, and that's how Mrs. Paris bundled and labeled their belongings, throwing out everything she possibly could.

Before her mother had taped up the last of the boxes, Maggie grabbed as many things as she could from Leah's room: books, the smallest of gadgets (Leah loved her gadgets), a Barbie puzzle, even a pair of sneakers—she hid them at the very bottom of the box. She still hadn't opened it when Julie came over for their first "playdate."

"What's in there?" Julie asked.

They had already explored the house, had a snack in the kitchen, fed Maggie's betta fish, and gone through pretty much everything in Maggie's room. Perhaps Mrs. Paris had been too thorough in her purging, because none of those activities had taken very long.

"Oh, it's just stuff from my old house."

"Let's open it," Julie said. She was on the floor, already pulling at the clear tape that held the top closed.

"No!" Maggie shouted. "Don't!"

She hadn't meant to yell like that, but Julie's eyes immediately welled up with tears.

Maggie got off the bed and joined her new friend on the floor. "I'm sorry." She put her hand on Julie's

66

back and rubbed it the way her mother used to when either of the girls was sad or tired or didn't feel well.

"No, I'm sorry," Julie said, blinking furiously.

"Wanna watch some TV?"

Julie smiled, and Maggie smiled back. There would be lots of time for more understanding, just not now. Maggie couldn't say for sure when she first told Julie about her sister, or even what she said, exactly, but when she did, she told her only what she had to, only what she told herself.

"The coach is such an ass," Julie said.

She kept her arms tightly around Maggie's shoulder. Coach Mac had given them two minutes to get back inside his office and finish the Red Cross video.

"It's OK, Jules. We can go back."

"No, we don't have to." They stayed crouched on the floor in the hall. "He should know better."

"Yeah, but he doesn't. Why should he?"

Julie was quiet. No one really knew about Leah. When Maggie had arrived, there had been some talk about something that happened to the new girl in her old town, maybe, bad or not so bad, but Maggie herself never talked about it. And after a while, without any more information, rumors faded and disappeared.

Julie, of course, knew. She knew Maggie had had an older sister, Leah, and that Leah had drowned in a pool in the condo park where they lived. That Leah had left her house when she wasn't supposed to and tried to swim alone. There was no lifeguard. There were a few people around but no one heard, or no one saw. No one was watching her, until it was too late. It was a long time ago. Leah was very young. Maggie was younger.

Julie knew that Maggie's parents had two more kids but their family was never the same.

She knew people now told Maggie things that they didn't tell anyone else, for reasons no one could really explain.

Beyond that, she was Maggie's best friend, nothing less.

"I'll stay out here with you, if you want," Julie offered.

"Nah, c'mon. I don't even know why the movie bothers me. I don't even remember much anymore."

"And it's probably over by now."

The girls walked back into the darkened room.

It was years before Maggie would even go near any substantial body of water. Until she agreed to step into a shower, her mother had to bathe her in only a few inches of tub water. Taking swim lessons for the first time when she was twelve years old was her father's idea.

By that time, Maggie had discovered her unusual "gift," and she had experienced how uncomfortable it made people, how lonely it made her feel. It was about this same time that her parents' silent anger, blame, love, and hate for each other became audible and unavoidable.

"She's terrified. What the hell purpose would it serve now?" Mrs. Paris's voice lifted high into the air that carried up the stairs, reverberated off the bedroom walls.

"So she can learn to swim. So she can live her life, Gail. Move on."

"What do swimming and living have to do with each other?" she shot back.

"It's about not being afraid."

"There are healthy fears, Don."

"Well, yours are not healthy."

Ultimately, Maggie's decision had more to do with hoping to heal her parents, and therefore herself, than with overcoming her fear of water, although in the end she achieved neither.

She began taking swim lessons at the Y. She was too young for adults-who-never-learned-to-swim class and too old for the Guppy or Minnow groups. Maggie ended up taking private swim lessons. Her teacher was a young woman named Ma'ayan.

"My name means water in Hebrew. Well, literally it means fountain or underground spring," she told Maggie. "Ma'ayan."

The water of the YMCA indoor pool was dank and dark, which suited Maggie just fine. It was exactly the unbeautifulness of it all that allowed Maggie to sit on the edge and dip her toes. There was no clear, sparkling blue, no sunshine and sparkle about it.

"*I'm* afraid of the water," Ma'ayan said. She wore a tight UV shirt over her bathing suit. She had curly brown hair pulled into a tight ponytail. She couldn't have been ten years older than Maggie.

Maggie braced herself for another confession.

"I didn't learn to swim until I went to college," Ma'ayan went on. "So I really understand how to teach it. None of it came naturally to me or too early for me to remember how to do it."

Maggie listened, waiting for the ridiculous, the pathetic, the miserable. People felt compelled to tell her the truth, and she felt oh-so-compelled to care, because she did.

"And I am a really good swimmer now. Every stroke perfect, but I am still scared."

"Scared of what?" Maggie asked. She let the water touch her ankles.

"Of drowning," Ma'ayan said.

No one said that around Maggie. No one used that word; no one ever connected Maggie's fear of swimming to drowning. Not out loud. Not to her face. Not in so many perfect words.

"I am too," Maggie said. "I am afraid if I go in the water, I might die."

"You would," Ma'ayan said, "if it were deep, or moving, or if you couldn't swim. That's why I'm going to teach you to swim."

And she did. It took five months, the first month of which they never got in the water past their ankles, never lifted their bottoms from the side of the pool. The second month Maggie felt the weight of the water slightly push against her thighs, then tighten the skin of her belly and shoulders with its cold. She let the water show its power, all its power and all its will. At the end of the third month, she held her breath, dunked under, and let the water take control of her life, so she could know what it was she was taking back. And in the fourth month, Maggie lifted her feet from the bottom and began to swim.

"Bend your elbow and let it pierce the surface, like a knife coming out of the water, taking the path of least resistance."

Swimming seemed to be all about the path of least resistance. Maggie kept her mind on that focus. It was about letting go.

"Now stretch your arm and let your hand slice the water. Don't fight it. Be part of it. You are entering into a temporary agreement with the forces of the water, a mutual respect."

Maggie pointed her fingers, used her feet like fins, and rocked her body from side to side, allowing the water to rush on each side. She felt the speed of movement like nothing she could feel on dry earth. It was like flying.

Learning to breathe was the hardest.

"Turn your head as little as possible, just to the point where the air meets the surface of the water. Trust that you are in control, that you can take in the oxygen and force out the water. Open your mouth just under your armpit."

They practiced for weeks, standing in the shallow end, holding on to the side and bending at the waist, dipping their faces into the water. Maggie felt the water come into her mouth. She felt it rush back out. The smoother she could make that transference, the faster she moved through the water. The more she could fool the water into believing she had gills for respiration, the smoother her stroke.

At the end of five months, Maggie tried out for the middle-school swim team but her parents didn't stop fighting. Instead, two years ago, they had spent a small fortune on fertility doctors, had another baby that turned out to be two babies, and for a while it looked like things might be better.

Eight

As predicted, and as was necessary for her plan, neither her mother nor father asked Maggie how she was getting back from the PSATs that morning. It had been an understanding since getting to high school that being responsible for your own transportation was part of the whole experience. If she needed a ride, she would ask. If she didn't ask, they wouldn't.

"Got your ID?"

Maggie nodded to her mother while downing her coffee.

"Calculator?"

Maggie nodded again. She didn't care about the PSATs. You weren't supposed to study for them, but of course, some kids did. Some kids had gotten tutors and taken an obscene number of practice PSATs, even though the *P* in PSAT stood for *practice*.

What Maggie cared about was getting there and being done when Nathan came to pick her up at noon. She cared that her parents were still planning on visiting Mrs. Paris's mother in Frenchtown, New Jersey, and were not expected back until evening, "at the earliest."

"Did you get a good night's sleep?" Her mother's final question.

"Yeah, Ma. Thanks," Maggie said, making sure not to catch her mother's eyes. It was better that way, not to directly look at each other, and it had been that way for a while.

Since Leah drowned? Just after?

When Maggie was in fifth grade, the school nurse sent her home with a raging red, goopy case of conjunctivitis. She wore two pairs of gloves as she pulled down on the skin just above Maggie's cheek. "How on earth did your mother let you come to school this morning?" the nurse said, shaking her head. She pulled the latex inside out, all five fingers at once. "You don't have to be a doctor. Just one look in your eyes and anyone would know."

Maggie finished all three sections of the PSAT before anyone else in the room did, walked to the front, and turned in her test packet. The proctor, who had been flipping through *Elle* magazine, looked up and offered Maggie the chance to recheck any answers or fill in the blank ones.

"No, thanks."

"Have a nice day, then," she said.

"You too," Maggie said, and she pulled open the heavy door. Nathan was waiting for her in the hall.

Leah

My sister, Maggie, and I like to play games, like clay face, and slapping faces, and motorcar. Our bodies are one. Our faces are one. I put my hands on my sister's face. Her skin is clay now, and whatever position I squeeze her into, she must try to keep it frozen that way, like hardened clay. We make funny faces, squinting our eyes and twisting our mouths, sucking in our cheeks or blowing them out. If we lie on opposite ends of the bed and press our feet together, one of us is the car, motor and all, making appropriate sounds of speeding up and braking, and the other is the driver, taking control of our lives, negotiating our way down the road.

Slapping faces is for when we are really bored — in the backseat of the car during a long trip, for instance. I let her slap me first, since she is younger and probably won't come right out and wallop me right off the bat. First of all, she's not that type, and second, if she does, then the rules of the game state that she must sit perfectly still and let me slap her back just as hard. We trade a few tiny pats for a while before one of us, usually me, ups the ante a little. It's a stupid game, and if our mother hears us from the front seat, she'll make us stop, so we have to be extra quiet.

"You go," I tell Maggie. She's not even five yet and does whatever I tell her. I close my eyes and feel the lightest tap on my cheek, almost a kiss.

But I am really bored today. I was bored the whole ride over to Grandma Ruth's in Frenchtown, even though I think it's funny because our name is Paris. I was bored the whole time we were there, and I got in big trouble for knocking over the orange juice in her fridge, where I apparently had no business being in the first *place. In front of all my cousins, I was given a time-out and not allowed to watch TV. And so I am extra bored on the long, long, long ride home, so I do it.*

I haul off and whack Maggie right across the face.

I watch as her eyes fly open and the imprint of my hand shows white against her red cheek. We look at each other. I can't forget her eyes.

I know I am going to get in big trouble now. Big trouble, like I always do, because they will always take Maggie's side and it won't matter what I say. No one will listen to me. My mom has been big on repercussions lately. She says I don't get any. Whatever they are I don't want them, but I bet hitting my little sister ranks right up there.

"What is going on back there?" First our mom asks, and then our dad, louder and more demanding, adding "the hell" as a modifier.

"Nothing," Maggie answers, and I know it is hard for her to talk because her throat is closing up with the tears that have sprung into her eyes, which only I can see. But she doesn't tell on me. My sister would never do that.

She doesn't say a thing.

Nine

Maggie watched Nathan closely as he drove, wondering what he would open up and tell her one day, maybe shortly, maybe later, but right now he wasn't talking, and she was grateful for that. She was oddly calm—considering what she was planning.

"Do you want to come in?" she asked him. They pulled around the circular driveway and Nathan threw the car into park.

"OK." He cut the engine.

"I can make us lunch. Are you hungry?"

Nathan smiled. "I can always eat."

"Yeah, my little brothers are like that."

"You have brothers. More than one?"

"Twins."

"Oh, right, you told me. Dylan and Lucas."

He remembered their names.

The door was unlocked, and the house was empty when they walked in. Maybe if it hadn't been such a beautiful day, but the sun was shining, clear and gentle, warm for late autumn. Maybe if the soft breeze hadn't been moving constantly above, keeping the air perfectly comfortable. Leaves still clinging, magnificent in their colors, red and gold, with no awareness that their end was so close. Maybe then Maggie would have been more apprehensive about what she hoped was about to happen, but it all seemed so perfect and right, as if the universe were confirming not only her plan but her motivation as well.

"Do you like turkey?" Maggie said with her head still in the fridge.

"Whatever's easy," Nathan answered.

Maggie really didn't watch enough music videos or beer commercials to know how to arch her back and stick out her rear end effectively anyway. Actually making lunch would take up precious time, so Maggie shut the fridge, turned around empty-handed, leaned back with her hands behind her back, and tipped her head up slightly.

"You can kiss me, you know."

It was a stupid thing to say, coy, and unreal, but she said it and it sounded pretty good, and Nathan looked startled but he stepped toward her.

"OK, then," he said.

It was a no-handed kiss. Maggie kept her arms pinned against the fridge behind her, and Nathan kept his at his side. They kissed for longer than was comfortable in that position, until Maggie took

Nathan's hand and started to pull him toward her room. He was quiet and not leading, but certainly not refusing.

"Maggie," he said, "what are you doing?"

She really didn't want to have to spell it out. That wasn't part of her plan. She just figured it would happen if she let it, if she made it happen. Didn't all boys want this?

Besides, she didn't have a plan B, so this was going to have to work.

What am I doing?

I am taking a boy into my room so he can have sex with me, so I won't be a virgin anymore and when the boy I really like comes home from college I can have sex with him.

Seriously?

The odd thing was that not only did this truth not occur to Maggie; it just didn't seem true anymore. Instead, it felt more like she was traveling into a new world that would belong only to her, where important decisions, even small decisions, would be her own. A world in which she would be alone, and she alone could choose whom to invite inside.

"Get out of the pool. Get back on the stair," Leah demanded of her little sister. She put her hands on her hips like their mother did, which looked silly to Maggie, little-girl fingers covering big yellow daisies. Leah was not the mother.

Maggie didn't move. The water felt good. It cooled her whole body; the smell of chlorine was inviting. The rays of sun bouncing off the surface looked like sparkles at a birthday party, glitter on a ballet costume.

"You're going to get in big trouble." Leah pulled out her final threat, and Maggie retreated.

Maggie walked back, sat down on the top step, and let the pool water wet the bottom of her suit. The cool water rushed between her legs and sent a shiver along her entire body. Maggie wouldn't be bad today. She never wanted to get into trouble. She wasn't that kind of kid sister, and she would never tattle or get her sister in trouble. Leah was counting on all those things.

"Anyway, I can too," Leah said.

"Can too, what?"

"Swim, dummy. I can too swim. I passed the deep-water test, and you know it," Leah said a little too loudly.

When Maggie looked over the chain-link fence that surrounded the pool, she knew exactly why. Just past the fence, and the grass, on the other side of the pavement, Meghan Liggett had come out of her house and was bending down, fiddling with something on her lawn, doing a worse job of pretending not to see Leah than Leah was doing pretending not to see her.

Maggie didn't know what she was doing, but she knew the basic mechanics and figured that would be enough to get her through. Every idiot in the world has sex at some point or another, and if you didn't count her now-probable PSAT scores, Maggie was certainly no idiot. Besides, her experience with Matthew had given her some idea of what to do.

"Are you sure this is a good idea?" Nathan said, his voice faltering between shallow breaths, between kisses, and his body pressing against hers, hers pressing back.

"It's fine," Maggie assured him. "It's a safe time."

Nathan pulled away. "A safe time?"

"Well, that didn't come out right."

It was about two o'clock, the hour when, at this particular time of the year, the sun broke at the surface, bent, and spread yellow across Maggie's room.

Everything looked golden, and it suddenly felt very bright, all too illuminated. They both sat up on top of the bed, the covers rumpled but still tucked tight.

"Maggie, I like you. I think I like you more than anyone I've ever been with."

The words "been with" stuck like an unexpected thorn. It hadn't occurred to Maggie that Nathan might have *been with* anyone before.

Nathan seemed more flustered. "I mean, I just thought we should . . . take it slow. I mean, not that I don't want to. And I know you say it's safe and all, but I wasn't thinking . . . I wasn't—"

Maggie opened her mouth so that air rushed in and made it sound like she was about to say something. Nathan stopped and waited, but Maggie was silent. It felt like a rejection and yet it didn't. It felt bad, and it felt like a relief. A lucid dream that was not working so lucidly. She woke up.

"I really like you, Maggie," he said again.

Funny she hadn't taken Nathan's feelings into consideration, or her own for that matter. It wasn't part of her plan, but now it was being offered. What had seemed clear was now, in this room, in this moment, in the space between two living human beings, suddenly understandable. Like the sun that crawls over the horizon and begins to light up a world that only moments earlier had been dark.

"I'm sorry. I mean, I don't know—" Maggie began.

She felt huge, too big for the bed, too exposed in the sunlight, and without enough air. She sat up and gripped her shirt where the top button had come undone.

Nathan swung his legs off the bed, hunching his shoulders. He looked uncomfortable, but he turned to her. "I'm the one that's sorry," he said. "I mean— that didn't come out right."

Maggie lifted her eyes to his and found him smiling, and then they were both laughing. "No, that *didn't* come out right," she said. She felt better. Laughing was good. "So do you want to eat something now?"

Nathan nodded. "Yeah, I'm starving."

If going to school was more bearable—besides seeing Julie in math class and at lunch and of course at practice, there, somewhere in the hall, might be Nathan. Every passing period, every excursion to the bathroom, could bring a sighting, and a sighting meant a smile, maybe a touch of the hand, maybe a kiss if no one was around—it also made being at home more bearable. Maggie owned something outside of her home life. Something that was secret, was hers, and was good.

She could still feel the arguments reverberate, even if her parents were long gone from the house: her dad at the gym, her mom and the boys out shopping.

Maybe it was all those porous surfaces, the wooden countertop, the paper towels that captured and held anger like a smell. But the kitchen especially held on to this morning's fight about the credit-card bill. *I told you to keep your receipts. How can you not know what this charge is? You did it. You did it. You did it.*

It was Saturday again. Swim practice was over, and Maggie had the house to herself—again. She was alone in the house—only she felt less alone than she had in a long time.

Julie's call trilled a Justin Bieber riff. It was an inside joke. It took Maggie a while to find her phone under a pile of clothing, and still-wet swim stuff is not a good place for a cell phone, but somehow it was still working.

"Whaja doing?" Julie asked.

"Nothing. Just hanging here."

"You sound happy. What's wrong?"

Maggie laughed. "I love you, too, Jules."

"I love you more. That's why I care," Julie said. "It's that just-some-boy, isn't it?"

It was, wasn't it?

Liking somebody who sounded happy when you called, who clearly dropped everything to pay attention to you, was actually a nice thing. Someone that you didn't have to pretend to bump into but was actually waiting around to see if you'd show up. It was really nice.

Julie never tolerated silence very well. "Maggie, why you are keeping this from me? You just don't want me to be all over it, do you? Because I was so anti-Matthew-the-shithead? Well, I can't help it."

What was wrong with feeling good? Nathan made her feel good. Made her feel that she was good.

"Yeah," Maggie whispered into her phone, though no one was home to hear her confession. "I like him, OK? You're right. I like Nathan. I like him a lot."

Leah

Grandpa Joel and Grandma Bunny are over, but I am in my room in a time-out and I hear them talking about me through the door. Sometimes the past, present, and future are all a jumble. And sometimes I think I hate my little sister and I think that things were better before she was born, even though my mother says I can't possibly remember anything from when I was that young. But I can. I remember everything. It's all the same. It's happening right now.

I get excited when I know my grandparents are coming. I am an excitable girl, my dad tells me. So maybe I was too rough with Maggie and I might have punched her in the stomach by mistake while we were playing.

"She needs to learn to control herself," my mom is telling Grandma Bunny. "A little time in her room isn't going to kill her."

Grandma Bunny talks loud, like she wants me to hear her while I am stuck in my room. Maggie is crying, first about the punch in the stomach and then about me getting punished. You think she'd be happy about that, but she's not.

Grandpa Joel talks now. "Sweetheart, we came all this way. You can discipline Leah all you want after we leave. C'mon, Gail, she's a little girl. She has the rest of her life to learn control; right now your mother wants to spoil her a little. We have presents for the girls."

I like that.

When the footsteps come near my door, I leap back up onto my bed and dive right into my pillow to hide my face. I don't want them to see my big wide smile. I feel my mother's hand on my back.

"OK, Leah, you can come out. Grandma Bunny and Grandpa Joel want to see you. We can talk about what happened later, OK?"

I take in a big gulp of air and answer into the pillow. "OK, Mom."

We walk out into the living room together, where everyone is waiting, and their eyes make me uncomfortable.

Grandma Bunny and Grandpa Joel brought us gifts, toys, like it's Christmas or our birthday, even though it's not. Not even close. They always do that, bring presents, every time they visit.

"Well, do you like it?" Grandma Bunny is asking me. I am surrounded by wrapping paper. Maggie has her paper folded into a little pile, which our mom loves, so she can reuse the wrapping. Sometimes I know I hate Maggie.

She seems to be very happy, hugging her new Flower

Fairy doll. Maggie collects them, and this time she got Jasmine, who is kind of blue and green, with wings like tree branches, and she's wearing sandals.

I got a fashion studio art kit sort of thing. It has the designer's table that lights up, so you can trace your model and then put clothes on her and color them in all different ways you want. They know I like to draw and make up fashions. I wanted this so badly, for so long, since I saw it on TV. I want to be happy. I want to like it. I want to make Grandma Bunny and Grandpa Joel happy like they are happy with Maggie. But I know I should really be back in my room being punished. I shouldn't be getting any presents at all.

I shrug my shoulders because I don't want to cry. "It's OK," I tell my grandma. "I guess I like it."

My mom is so mad at me now. I can see it in her face, and I don't even have to look at her. Now she really thinks I am bad. Now, in this present time (get it?), she knows it.

Ten

"I have a scar on my chest," Nathan told her.

It was two weeks past the PSATs. But for Maggie, in many ways it felt like a new lifetime. Being at Nathan's house, in his room, was already familiar. How had that happened so quickly?

Nathan moved to unbutton his shirt but stopped. "All down my chest and under my arm."

Should she make him aware, level the playing field, let him in on her secret before it was too late?

"You do?"

Nathan nodded. "When I was little, I was standing on a chair at the stove. I wanted to make real oatmeal. So I reached over and stuck a wooden spoon into the pot to see if the water was ready. I tipped it right over. It spilled all over me and soaked my pajamas. That was the worst part—that it kept burning because my pajamas got wet and stuck to my skin."

She didn't look away, but Maggie was quiet.

Nathan's parents were downstairs, but maybe with so many children, they weren't that interested in what any particular one was doing at any particular time, especially if he was a teenage boy and he was home safe and not out driving. In any case, Maggie and Nathan lay on his bed, the blankets rumpled from their kissing and the sheet twisted at the bottom from not having been made for most likely several days. Their clothing stayed on, only their mouths exploring what was inside, what was hidden and so tantalizing that Maggie's whole body shook. Nathan's older brother and his friend, footsteps in the hall and a bouncing ball and a quick argument about last night's game, had interrupted them. They sat up.

"I was in the hospital for two weeks. It was the most painful thing I've ever felt. And ever felt since. Burn scars are different than other scars, you know. They are ugly."

Very slowly Maggie reached over, put her hands where Nathan's were, and began to unbutton the top of his shirt. His collar opened, and she let her fingers drop to the next button. She slipped it outside its hole and made her way down his shirt without saying a word.

She spread the fabric of his shirt and exposed his skin to the bath of yellow light.

"It's not so bad," she said.

"I know it is."

It wasn't. The skin was taut and red in streaks, like anger. It was smoother than his other skin, without hair or pores, and twisted in places it shouldn't twist, but it wasn't ugly at all.

"Can I touch it?" Maggie asked. "Does it hurt?"

"No. It was a long time ago; it's healed," Nathan said. "I mean, yes, you can touch it."

Maggie let her fingers spread across Nathan's chest, his ribs, his skin, across the damage that boiling water had done. He wasn't big, like a football player, nothing like Matthew, but Nathan's body felt different from hers. Slight but solid, male. The surface of his scar was bumpy, hard and soft at the same time. Maggie let her head nestle in that spot just under Nathan's shoulder and just inside his arm, where she fit perfectly, and where for the first time that she could remember, she allowed the weight of her body to be supported and the weight of her mind to rest.

The girls were shivering on the bulkhead, listening to Coach Mac give out the upcoming holiday-break practice schedule: basically, there would be no break for the swim team.

"OK, ladies. Hit the showers. Eat a big dinner;

get your protein. Get your eight hours of Z's, and be here at six a.m. tomorrow. Oh, and if anyone is late—any*one*—the whole team does IM drills. Fifteen hundred meters."

There were appropriate groans and the patter of wet rubber pool shoes slapping the floor, heading to the locker room, the swell of weekend conversations. It was Friday. Even with the practice schedule, it was still vacation, and the excitement was palpable.

Maggie and Nathan had been meeting from time to time: at a football game and then heading off to walk the cross-county trails behind the school; at the Landmark Diner for swim-season-forbidden fries. Wherever they ended up, they ended up kissing, touching, looking closely at the other's face and body.

And yet it was Thanksgiving vacation. Maggie had planned so long for this break.

"What are you doing this weekend?" Julie asked as she leaned to the side and yanked at a knot in her wet hair. Julie's hair was curly, thick, and if she didn't comb it out right away it would dry into Medusa-like coils.

"Nothing," Maggie said. "How about you?"

"The usual. My grandparents are eating with us tonight. Wanna come for dinner? You know they love you, and it would take the focus off me."

"I don't know. Maybe." Maggie stuffed her school clothes into her bag, sat down, and waited for Julie to finish.

"Oh, I see. You're waiting to see if Nathan boy is available?" Julie smiled.

"Not exactly," Maggie answered. Sometimes she understood why girls cut themselves. What seemed so stupid, so obvious and pathetic even, made sense. The pain is real, and even if it doesn't feel good, it feels right. She had wanted Matthew for so long. How would she ever know if she didn't at least try?

Julie stopped brushing, righted herself, and held her comb like a gun at her hip.

"What, Maggie? What are you thinking? Please tell me it's not about Matthew. Oh, please, you're kidding."

"Well—"

Julie sat down on the bench beside her friend. The steam from the showers remained separated from the cold air in the locker room and settled like fog.

"Matthew is a big ass," Julie said. "I am truly

sorry to be the one to tell you. But this Nathan seems nice, and the fact that he's actually into you is a real bonus, don't you think?"

Was he? Surely as soon as Nathan really got to know her, he'd figure out she wasn't worth the trouble.

It was all so ridiculous. She could hardly remember why she liked Matthew in the first place, but the sense of anxiety didn't go away. It was like a riding a train that was going in two directions—one toward the unknown and the other straight into a stone wall. Wasn't it better to crash on your own volition than sink slowly against your will?

It was hilarious, really.

"What's so funny?" Julie asked.

"Nothing. I know you're right. It's just that I was so crazy about him last year, and that's not really that long ago. I never really gave Matthew a chance."

"A chance? A chance for what, Maggie? He's got a girlfriend. And besides, he's a dick."

"Nothing. You're right. I don't care. I won't even think about him again."

"So c'mon." Julie bent over and resumed working on her hair. When she stood up again, she said, "Look, you're coming to my house tonight. Period."

Julie's parents were larger than life. They fought out loud; they laughed even louder. They kissed each other frequently, sometimes smack on the lips. The whole family ate with zeal and left the dishes in the sink for the next morning if the conversation was good. No subject seemed to be off-limits at the dinner table. It was nothing like her own home, and Maggie loved it there.

Everyone talked over everyone else, loudly, excitedly. Confessions and accusations were common. Exaggerations, enhancements, and contradictions flew across the table, knocking over the salt and pepper shakers, rattling the candlesticks, especially when Mrs. Bensimon's parents were visiting. The Bensimons were Jewish, and tonight was Friday night, Shabbat dinner at Julie's house.

"Oh, Ma, for Christ's sake, we have company." Mrs. Bensimon was referring to Maggie, who had been sitting quietly through the entire argument, enjoying every minute.

Julie's grandma Bobbie, Mrs. Bensimon's mother, turned her attention to Maggie. "She's not company. Maggie's family here. What's the matter with you, Deborah?"

"Of course, Ma, but not everybody's interested in the functioning of your alimentary track, especially not at the dinner table. Speaking of which, have you been taking that supplement I gave you?"

Julie's mother was a dietician.

"What supplement?"

"Ma, I brought home all those free samples. I put them right on your kitchen counter, remember? Last week? When Dad had his car serviced?"

"Last week?" Grandpa Bob didn't look up from his chicken when he spoke. "I didn't have my car serviced last week."

"Yes, you did, Dad."

"I think I would remember if I had my car serviced, sweetie."

"You never give me free samples."

"Ma, I did. They'll keep you regular."

"I haven't been regular since the Korean War," Grandma Bobbie said. Their real names were Robert and Barbara, Bob and Bobbie. Grandma Bobbie and Grandpa Bob.

"I lost my cell phone again," Julie's older brother, Jason, chimed in. He probably didn't want to hear about the success rate of his grandmother's morning rituals much either.

Mr. Bensimon, Julie's dad, walked in from the kitchen. "Again, Jason? How many times is this?"

"We have insurance, don't we?"

"That's not the point."

"Third time," Julie offered.

"It still costs fifty dollars."

"And it's just irresponsible. It's time you learned the value of something."

Mr. and Mrs. Bensimon traded admonishments, none of which seemed to bother Julie's brother in the least. Doing something wrong didn't make you wrong in this family. It just added to the color and drama of the conversation.

"I've never lost my cell phone," Julie added. "Doesn't that mean I should *get* fifty dollars?"

"Did you check the lost-and-found at school?" Maggie managed to slip a tiny remark into the mix. She didn't realize her question would cause the whole family to start giggling.

"What?" Maggie asked, smiling.

"Well"—Grandma Bobbie prepared to launch like a liftoff at NASA—"when Grandpa Bob and I were first married"—she looked right at Maggie—"and you can consider him your grandpa, too," she went on, "we didn't have a pot to piss in."

"Ma—"

"We weren't that poor, Deborah," Grandpa Bob interrupted.

"Oh, really, Mr. Big Shot—"

"Just get to the story, Grandma."

Everyone had a comment, and that carried on during the whole story. Not a sentence or two went uninterrupted, unchallenged, or unembellished, and by the time Mrs. Bensimon's mother got to the end, everyone was exhausted from laughing, including Maggie. The gist of it was that Grandma Bobbie needed a pair of gloves, and, not being able to afford a nice pair, she walked into some fancy department store with her husband, headed straight up to lost-and-found and explained that she had lost a pair of leather gloves.

"What color are they?" the woman behind the counter asked.

"Brown," said Barbara, who was not yet Grandma Bobbie.

"Black," said her husband at the exact same time.

"Brownish black," Barbara said firmly, and the woman pulled out a pair and asked if these were the missing gloves.

"Well, let's see." Barbara slipped them on and held them out in the light. "No, I don't think these are them. Got anything else back there?"

By this time in the story, tears of laughter were

streaming down her cheeks, taking half of her thick foundation and leaving a trail of black mascara behind.

This is what family is, Maggie knew, a collection of stories, half-truths, and raw honesty, a conglomeration of conflicting memories that somehow all add up. A place where no one is afraid to say what's on their mind; no one is afraid to tell the truth. Or lie, for that matter, because it hardly made a difference. Love is love is truth is love.

Leah

Maggie didn't come to my funeral. They wouldn't let her. They didn't even tell her about it. She was too young, they felt. It will just confuse her. *I heard them talking, but, of course, parents protect themselves and pretend they are protecting their children.*

Sometimes I wonder if Maggie even knew I had died, or if she sat waiting for me — if she's sitting there still — downstairs in the den, where we kept all our toys, our books, all the little dolls we made out of paper and felt and colored with Magic Markers. That afternoon, Maggie sat for hours, not moving until our next-door neighbor, Mrs. Tate, went down there herself.

"You can't stay down here all afternoon," Mrs. Tate told her. "You need to come upstairs and eat something."

"No," Maggie said. She faced the wall of glass doors that led out to the backyard, where we used to sit cross-legged in the grass and play clapping games, like Miss Mary Mack and Itsy Meanie Teeny Eeny.

"Now, Maggie," Mrs. Tate said, "I insist. You've been waiting down here since everyone left for the—"

"For where?" Maggie looked up. "Where did everyone go?"

"Well, that's for your mother to talk to you about." And Mrs. Tate turned on her heels, back up the stairs. The swinging door into the kitchen banged shut.

They were all at my funeral, dressed in dark colors, faces red and swollen, and Maggie was alone. She was alone in a way she had never been before. At the service nobody talked much, except for the reverend. He talked a lot and said nothing at all. The room was hot—too much air, too much carbon dioxide. The reverend went on and on. He read some poetry, the 23rd Psalm, and then he talked some more.

"OK, Maggie. This is it." Mrs. Tate had trouble with stairs, but she made her way down again. This time holding a plate of chocolate-chip cookies, warm from the oven. "With raisins," she offered. "Your favorite."

Maggie got up from the floor.

"Good girl," Mrs. Tate said.

She took a cookie. It melted in her mouth. "I'm not a good girl," Maggie said. The cookie was sweet and delicious. I know it was, and it made her instantly thirsty, but she didn't ask for a drink.

"Oh, nonsense. Here, take another one."

Maggie stuffed another cookie into her mouth. It was hard to chew; her mouth was dry, her voice crumbly. "That's why they don't want me there."

"That's not true at all, Maggie. Why do you make up stories like that?"

I always thought that I was the bad one, the one who got in trouble, so I knew what Maggie was feeling, but there was nothing I could do about it now.

Eleven

When Maggie was at the height of making herself available to Matthew last year, most of her time was actually spent waiting.

She waited for him to text her. Waited to bump into him at parties. Waited for his sister, Jennifer, to invite the girls over to work on another school project so Matthew could say "See ya" again, but it didn't happen. She waited as if it were an art form, and this Thanksgiving break—other than swim practice, eating, and sleeping—Maggie perfected it. Over Thanksgiving break, Nathan texted dozens of times and even called her house phone, but with all the family obligations she claimed to have—of which there were none—Maggie managed to remain home doing nothing other than going to the pool and waiting.

Saturday morning, after an early practice, Maggie sat in front of the TV with her computer on her lap, the volume muted. She intermittently checked her Facebook and popped another Frosted Mini-Wheat into her mouth. The rest of her family was still sleeping, even the boys. The house was perfectly quiet but for the ticking of the kitchen clock, a square blue face painted with the White Rock girl gazing into the surface of a gentle pond.

Maggie used to pretend—and sometimes still did—that she *was* the White Rock girl, with her little fairy wings that sprouted like tree branches. It would worry her, though, that those disproportionate tiny wings would be way too small and weak, and what good would it be to have wings so small and so useless? Maggie tried to concentrate on her TV show, a dog video on YouTube, and her reading homework for honors English. Then Matthew's name popped up as a "friend online" in a short list at the right-hand bottom of her screen, and a few seconds later he sent her a message.

Whassup?

And just like that, her heart broke into loud thumps. Matthew was leaving that afternoon, later, he explained, but had a little time just before he headed back upstate. Did she want to meet him? Maggie immediately agreed, expecting somehow that wholeness could come by tearing herself apart.

As a gift, when she finished her swim lessons— not only learned to swim but turned out to be exceptional—her father had planned a trip for the whole family to Club Med, where Maggie would get to swim with the dolphins. Her dad knew she had always loved dolphins. Didn't she watch the *Free Willy* DVD over and over? Of course, Willy was a killer whale, but what's the difference, and all girls love dolphins and horses, don't they? He wanted to make her happy, and he wanted to heal his family.

Lucas and Dylan were only two years old when they all boarded a plane for Punta Cana, in the Dominican Republic.

The twins had gotten past their infant stage,

when they did nothing but cry and eat and poop, and were actually getting kind of cute. They were finally living up to their birthright, their birth *burden,* to overshadow the memory of Leah's death. Besides, Mrs. Paris had worked hard on getting her figure back, which is why she agreed to this trip at all. Body Pump and Inner Strength classes had been her religion for the last four months. Vacations were good by definition, right?

But by Wednesday, the day of the dolphin excursion, Mrs. Paris was sick with diarrhea. She put the twins in the full-day babysitting, and thirteen-year-old Maggie and her dad headed out on the open-air bus alone.

"The guy at the desk said it's a twenty-minute ride, didn't he?" Mr. Paris leaned close to ask his daughter. It was hard to hear, between the wind and the sound of the bus motor. They had booked an excursion to Dolphin Island. The hotel arranged everything, including the bus ride.

Maggie shouted back, "I think so, Dad, but he had a strong accent. I'm not sure."

"Hmm, French or Spanish?"

"What? I can't hear you, Dad."

He didn't hear her either. He rubbed her back and asked, "So are you excited?"

It was even louder now that they had hit the highway. She tried to yell out her answer, but she gave up. Yes, she *was* excited. After all, dolphins were kind of Maggie's animal guide, weren't they? Mammals that swam, breathed air but lived underwater, and what about all those TV specials where dolphins were reported to have rescued people or led boats to safety or fended off shark attacks?

"In the wild," the Dominican dolphin trainer explained, once everyone was standing in the murky, forty-by-twenty-five-foot floating enclosure, surrounded by slimy algae-caked fencing, "a dolphin might live thirty to thirty-five years. They have a lot of natural enemies out there, including humans."

Everyone else was smiling, Maggie noticed. The young girls and their mothers, especially, could hardly contain themselves as the dolphins swam back and forth, around the line of people in which Maggie and her dad stood shivering. As luck would have it, it was the one day, the one hour, in Punta Cana that the sun had not come out since they had arrived in the Dominican. When one of the two dolphins, apparently insane with repetitive stress behavior, swam close to the humans in its circle, everyone was supposed to put out their hands and let their fingers graze the top of the massive animal. A girl or two squealed each time.

"But here, safe, at Dolphin Island," the man went on. He stood atop the wooden platform that surrounded the tank, whistle poised in his mouth, and a bucket of dead fish beside him. He smiled, though no one seemed to be listening, and he tried to make eye contact with all the tourists. Then he looked right at Maggie. "Here, our dolphins live only half that life span on average." She would remember that moment as solidifying the existence of her power. The moment she came to believe in the unpleasant and uncontrollable nature of truth telling.

"Can we hold on to their fins?" a boy asked, even though the introductory video had already explained that hanging on the dolphins was not allowed.

He fiddled with the large plastic skull charm he had hanging around his neck from a leather cord. He clearly hadn't taken off *any and all jewelry.* Maggie's hair whipped around her face due to the lack of even a ponytail clip. This boy was annoying her.

"You know"—the trainer kept his eyes on Maggie; he looked sad, despite his overly cheerful voice—"no matter how many times we tell everyone not to hang on the animals, someone always does." His English was perfect, and his Spanish accent made it sound like music, so it took the boy a while to realize that he was being reprimanded.

The trainer let the whistle fall from his mouth. He stopped reaching into his bucket of fish. "Day after day, four times in the morning and three times in the afternoon, these two dolphins perform for rich tourists like you. They will jump up into the air and balance on their tails so they can have one tiny dead fish dropped in their mouths."

The crowd shifted uncomfortably. Maggie was certain he was looking right at her again.

"In the ocean, these animals would normally swim hundreds"—he paused and repeated—"hundreds of miles a day, hunt for their own food, and find their own companions. They are extremely smart animals. Here, they swim in circles, over and over and over, so that I can take home a paycheck and feed my family for a month with what you will go home and pay for a new video game."

"All right, all right," the boy responded. It was hard to tell exactly what he was paying attention to, but *video game* seemed to register with him.

"I think, ladies and gentlemen, that if I were a dolphin, I would prefer *not* to live than to live like this, and yet, here I am, holding the bucket and blowing this whistle."

"I think we should go now," Mr. Paris said, but nobody moved.

Another trainer hurried out onto the deck. With a big smile, he took the whistle and the bucket and gleefully took over the rest of the show. Maggie hoped the first man wouldn't lose his job. She worried about his family, but when it was her turn, Maggie took her place on the partially submerged metal platform. Then, on command, one of the dolphins rose out of the water, paused for a moment, leaning his massive body against hers, and pressed his bottlenose against her cheek in what was to simulate affection, while someone on the deck snapped the photograph and then tried to sell it to Maggie and her father as they were leaving.

"But don't you want to buy a photograph of your daughter getting kissed by a dolphin?" a very pretty girl in a bikini asked in perfect English.

"No, *gracias,*" Maggie answered before her dad could say anything.

But then Matthew wasn't there, where he'd said he'd meet her, by the front of the school, near the track. Matthew James was a no-show. A few minutes later, a text buzzed into her pocket telling her he couldn't make it. He had to get on the road back up to Albany. His ride was leaving early. *Sorry, Abbe.* She figured he'd meant to spell *Babe* but hadn't bothered to even look at the screen while he was typing.

He was such a jerk, just like Julie had said.

What did she call Matthew? A shit-for-brains? Shithead? A douche bag? The familiar comfortable feeling of discomfort rose up from Maggie's feet, settled in her belly, and then flew around in her brain. It didn't feel good, but on the other hand, it felt just right.

Twelve

"You so waited all week for him, didn't you?" Julie asked. She had just finished her race, coming in third in her heat, breaststroke, and breaking her personal best. She was feeling pretty good. Together, Julie and Maggie sat on the metal bleachers in their pajama bottoms and Uggs, their hair wet, their eye sockets ringed by goggle suction.

"No, not *all* week. Wednesday I went to the mall with my mom, remember?"

"Nice," Julie said. "Good job."

"Did you just roll your eyes? You know I hate it when you roll your eyes." Maggie's race was being announced. "I gotta go."

"No, not at all. I never roll my eyes," Julie said. "Good luck. You don't need it, but good luck."

When Maggie turned back around, Julie had pulled her knees up to her chest and had wrapped her arms around her legs. When she caught Maggie's gaze, Julie rolled her eyes as dramatically as she could.

Maggie stood on the starting block, looking out onto the water. The lane markers rocked slightly on the surface, from the race before, but other than that, the water was silent, coaxing. She looked once toward the bleachers. Her dad was there. Her teammates. Julie gave her the thumbs-up. But no Nathan.

Maggie crouched, her hands gripping the base of the block. She heard the commands and then nothing else. She jerked her body forward into the air. Her fingertips touched the surface first, piercing it and sliding inside. She would win the race and the one after that. Her team would take second in the relay, which would give them enough points to win the meet and get one step closer to the state semifinals. Everyone would be celebrating, except the other team, of course, and though not many students would be listening, the principal would report the good news on the morning announcements. Maggie wanted to believe that even though he had stopped calling and texting, Nathan would be sitting somewhere in class and hear of her achievements through the loudspeaker.

Maggie prayed that Meghan Liggett would just go back into her dumb-old house already. She had a bad feeling about this as she sat on the pool stairs, as Leah had directed her to do.

People always claim to have known something bad was going to happen before it happened. They talk about premonitions and foreboding, but if they really knew, why did they let it happen? And why would they then admit something like that? If you could have known beforehand, you would have stopped it. And if you didn't, you would have to live a lifetime with that knowledge. Why would anyone ever want to admit that?

But there Meghan was, just puttering around on her green, green lawn in her purple Gap shorts and matching T-shirt. And even though Maggie herself had invoked Meghan to entice Leah outside the apartment, Maggie also understood this to be big trouble.

Before Leah stepped into the pool, Maggie remembered thinking—realizing for the first time—how wrong it was to want someone you didn't like, someone who didn't like you. Maggie realized this was her first real *grown-up* thought, and it had come too late to do anything about it.

And just as Maggie was processing the newness of a thought that was so profound and complex, Leah went into the water. She didn't step in or slowly submerge one body inch at a time, as they sometimes did together.

Toes, ankles, shins.

Shins, knees.

Shins, knees, thighs.

Shins, knees, thighs, tushy.

No, Leah dove in off the first step, and when she poked her head back out, her hair was slicked back and long down her back. Water trickled down her nose, and the sun reflected off her wet cheeks, and Maggie remembers thinking her sister was the prettiest, most special big sister in the whole world.

If Meghan Liggett wasn't jealous by now, she should be.

"I'm not stupid, Maggie," Nathan said. At Maggie's request, they walked around the track, close but not touching.

Yes, he wanted to see Maggie again, but he was hurt. She had avoided him all Thanksgiving break. He didn't know what he had done to deserve that. When she saw him in the cafeteria Monday morning, Nathan reluctantly agreed to talk.

"My dad has this saying," Nathan started. He was prepared.

"Yeah?"

"Yeah, well, my dad has a lot of sayings, and he's always saying them and some of them make a lot of sense."

"Well, tell me one that doesn't make sense first, then," Maggie said softly, as softly as she could.

By this point they were on the far side of the football field, the school, the tennis courts, and far from anybody who happened to be out at this time. Without saying so, they both slowed their pace, nearly to a stop.

"OK," Nathan said. "It is what it is."

"Huh?"

"That's the saying. He says it a lot. He says, 'It is what it is.' And I tell him that doesn't make any sense. It's redundant and meaningless."

Maggie laughed. "It's just like saying, 'Get over it.' Deal with it. It's not going to change. It is what it is."

"Like 'Fuck it,'" Nathan added.

"Yeah, 'Fuck it.'"

Nathan stopped. "But you don't strike me as a 'Fuck it' kind of girl. So why did you stop talking to me? What happened?"

She wouldn't tell him, not the whole of it. There are certain ways to lie without lying at all, though it wasn't telling the truth either. Lies by omission. Telling a version of the story that sticks to the facts, like syrup running back down the inside of the jar.

"I got overwhelmed by practice and my parents fighting all the time," she offered. All true.

"I didn't know," Nathan said.

"And the coach has a lot of expectations. A lot of them on me." Maggie tried kissing him, or she

115

thought about kissing him, hoping she looked kissable and he would respond.

"So what's the other saying?" she asked him.

"What other saying?"

"The other saying your dad told you."

"Oh." Nathan pulled her tightly toward him. He returned her almost kiss, his lips cold from the air and warm, both, and they started walking again. Side by side, bumping hips, brushing arms. "He says, 'Never sell a good thing twice.'"

A television advertisement for some automobile or new food processor came to mind, with confetti and balloons, and then, finally, she got it: *Never sell a good thing twice.*

"Oh, you mean, *you*. Don't sell yourself. Twice," Maggie said. "Don't sell yourself more than once, because once should be enough? Because you're worth it, right?"

"Right. And this is twice already. I can't go for three."

Maggie told him, "You won't have to."

Nathan let his hand drift back and reach for hers. He held it out and waited. It was the quietest, kindest invitation.

"It must be nice to know you're worth it," she said.

"Huh?"

"Nothing." Maggie took his hand, wrapping her fingers between his, and held it tight.

Lucid dreaming had become easier. By the time she came home from practice, ate dinner, and stayed up doing homework—well past the hour her body wanted to sleep and dreaming was within reaching distance—Maggie would lay her head down and had to spend most of her concentration trying *not* to fall asleep, not yet.

Not so fast, she willed her mind.

But now, instead of creating scenarios that she wished would come true, she dreamed of moments she had spent with Nathan, moments that had already come true. She relived them, retold them, until she could feel them again. The one or two she liked best, she kept repeating, like a favorite book on the nightstand.

Behind her eyes, the images were not made of light waves or words, not sound the way sound travels through the air in waves, but something beyond language and beyond sight. Pure feeling. Maggie moved her hand to her belly and felt her own skin, soft and, between her legs, warm. The story began as memory. Nathan walked up behind

117

her, turned her around, and placed his hands on the sides of her face, his fingers touching her neck, pulling her toward him. When she felt his lips on her forehead, then the bridge of her nose so that now she could smell him, the cotton of his clothing and the scent of his breath, a sensation drove through her body, all beginning and ending between her thighs. Nathan moved beside her, keeping one hand on her face and putting the other on the small of her back, so she felt trapped and supported. She felt both possessed and more powerful than she had ever felt before. He came to lie beside her, face-to-face.

When he pulled her to him, Maggie could feel the heat of his mouth on hers. She could feel the pressure of her own hand and hear her shallow breathing quicken.

In those words beyond language, Nathan told Maggie he loved her, and she felt it wholly as it flooded her entire body.

"You're not eating," Mr. Paris commented. Maggie's dinner plate looked untouched.

"I'm waiting for Mom to come in."

Mrs. Paris still had not sat down. They could hear her scraping plates, moving dishes around.

"Mom, come and sit down," Maggie called into the kitchen.

"Be in in a minute. Just want to get these pots soaking. You know how brown sugar sticks. It's something about the sugar caramelizing in the high heat. If I don't get it soaking, it will never come clean."

So her parents were fighting again.

Her mother's voice arched in that false, high-pitched, overly explanatory way. Her father wouldn't make eye contact when he talked, but he spoke as if nothing were wrong. Maggie wondered if they really thought they were fooling anyone. Or just themselves.

"Maggie, just eat. You know how your mother is," Mr. Paris said.

A pot banged in the sink.

The boys had already finished, or hardly eaten, and darted from the table, diving onto the couch that acted as a separation to the living room. They were allowed to turn on the TV but had to keep the volume down. Lucas popped his head up with Dylan right beside him.

"Love Maggie is in," he said.

Dylan finished: "Why that is she won't eat."

Mr. Paris raised his eyebrows, first at the boys,

then at Maggie. But he seemed happy to have something to redirect the tension away from him.

"You have a boyfriend, Maggie?" Mr. Paris asked.

"No, Dad. I don't have boyfriend. It's just a boy I know."

Mr. Paris smiled. "You kids. I don't know what's changed. When did it become uncool to be dating?"

"Nobody dates, Dad."

"I believe you. I just think it's sad, that's all. Love is a beautiful thing."

Maggie thought her mother might have clanked another plate into the dishwasher with a bit of extra aggression, but she couldn't be sure.

Mrs. Paris appeared in the doorway between the kitchen and the dining room. She had a wet dish towel flung over her shoulder, just in case anyone should doubt the work she had been doing. She put her hand on her hip.

Mrs. Paris looked at her husband, then at the heads of her two twin boys peering over the couch, and then at her remaining daughter. "Well, Maggie, invite him over for dinner sometime. Even if he's not your boyfriend, he must have to eat," Mrs. Paris said.

Thirteen

The girls' swim team was granted permission to miss the second half of last period in order to get on the bus and make the two-hour drive to the Wilton YMCA. Large meets were, at least, less boring. There was more going on. Usually a sports store set up shop in a corner, selling bathing suits, caps, and goggles. Music might be pumped in. Hot dogs cooked. Cookies sold. There were swimmers in all stages of chlorine saturation and in various colorful outfits. A lot of the girls were decorating their pool shoes with plastic fruit or toy animals, which flopped around with every step.

Maggie walked around between races, imagining how she would report it back to Nathan, which things he would find funny or interesting. She had located the most remote toilet right away, a single handicapped bathroom on the opposite end of the building, which, thankfully, someone forgot to lock.

"I'm sorry I can't be there," Nathan had told her. He skipped last period to walk her to the bus. "But, here, take this."

Maggie held out her hand. "What is it?"

"It's something of me, so I can be there with you when you win. Don't open it until you win."

121

"And what if I don't?" A bunch of faces were already looking out the windows of the bus. "What if I don't win?"

"You will. Then you'll open it."

Her first event was the 800 free. She took second, a good seventeen points for the team. A win, certainly. Maggie dried off her hands and reached into her swim bag for the brown-paper package Nathan had given her. Underneath the first wrapper was a rectangle of aluminum foil, and inside that, covered in cellophane, was a perfectly shaped, perfectly baked loaf of oatmeal chocolate-chip banana bread. A small yellow Post-it note was pressed on top, with *A piece of me for you* written in boy scrawl. And just as she thought of needing one, Maggie noticed a white plastic knife wedged on the side, which brought an enormous smile to her face.

"It's looking good." Julie bounced over to where Maggie was sitting cross-legged on the floor in the Y lobby. "Ooh, what's that?"

"It's banana bread."

"Yum, it's all good. And hey, with your win, we only have to place in the four-by-one-hundred medley relay and we go to the state semifinals, and if we win those, we go to the state finals, and then to

Nationals—and that's in Florida. Cecily is already talking about getting us a side trip to Disney."

"That's cool. Wanna slice?"

"Of course," Julie said. She picked up the Post-it. "Nathan? My God, he bakes, too?"

"Apparently so." Maggie thought about a little boy burning himself at the stove who now makes banana bread, and she smiled.

"Oh, my God. With chocolate chips."

"Umm, I know."

"You deserve this, Maggie." Julie licked the crumbs from her fingers. "OK, maybe you don't— but I do."

"I know."

Since the backstroke begins in the water, it is always the first leg of the relay, to avoid a second swimmer landing on anyone's head. After that, the relay is arranged by speed: breast, fly, free. Maggie had the last leg, the fastest time and stroke: front crawl.

She watched Natasha Beard coming in a few lengths behind the lead swimmer. Natasha had a powerful kick. It propelled her out of the water, her arms arching, her mouth wide open to suck in that beautiful air, but there would be seconds to catch up, fractions of a second to pass. The sounds across the water were deafening: people were not only cheering but screaming. One team would advance; one would see the end of their swim season.

The key was to launch yourself off the starting blocks at the exact perfect moment that your teammate touched the automatic touch pad. A second too early and you risk disqualification; a second late could cost the race.

The splashing became louder, each water molecule spinning, shaken from its principle and sent off into space, longing to return to become one again. It was as if Maggie could hear each one calling to her, pleading with her, telling her when to dive, propelling her through the water.

The ride home was quiet. Coach Mac asked everyone to save their celebrations and focus on what they needed to do to win the state semifinals. Most of the girls were exhausted at this point, leaning their heads against the window or one another. It was nearly ten p.m. Some of the team had been allowed, with prior written permission, to go home with their parents, but most of the girls rode the bus. The next meet, which would leave only six teams competing in the finals, was less than a week away.

Maggie had told her dad he could drive straight home. She told him she had a ride. She knew Nathan would be waiting for her in the high-school parking lot, and he was.

The darkness of late fall pressed against the car windows, but inside, it felt cozy, the engine vibrating steadily, the blowers warming the air. Nathan kept his eyes on the road, but he reached over, feeling for Maggie's hand. When he found it, he gave it a squeeze and held on.

Maggie told him, "The bread was delicious."

"I knew you'd win."

"How do you know? How do you know I didn't just lose and eat it anyway?"

"Oh, everyone heard already. Tweets and texts, you know. But thanks. I'm glad you liked the banana bread."

"With chocolate chips."

"Why not?" Nathan smiled.

They turned onto Maggie's block and Nathan swung the car into the driveway. Maggie watched. He took a moment, then shifted into park; another second and he cut the engine. When he turned to kiss her, Maggie was already there. She let her face, her lips, her body, melt into his. It was part

fatigue, part excitement, but another part life —
living, being alive, being connected — and she
wanted more. She wanted it more deeply. She
wanted it to last, to obliterate everything that came
before and maybe after.

Maggie groped Nathan's body, keeping her eyes
shut as if blind and only seeing for the first time.
She reached inside his shirt and drew a map. She let
her fingers slide across his chest, his shoulders, the
dip of his belly, the shadow of parts hidden below,
touching every surface, absorbing him, trying to
attach her skin to his, trying to heal his wound with
hers. Nathan groaned softly and did not protest.
Instead, he responded in kind, and with urgency
and gentleness, and that night, Maggie found it all
easily beautiful, and she understood immediately
why this had not worked before.

Maggie watched the world change around her,
simply because she had been changed, and it made
her happy. It was as if the edges had softened, the
hardness of the Formica desks, the harshness of the
fluorescent lights in the ceiling, the sharp voice of
her history teacher.

Maggie sat, content in a way she had never felt
before. She had separated herself, truly marked a

break from her parents, from all those in charge. She had joined the ranks — not of the adults, per se, but of those just a bit older than her. The secret they had once kept was now hers, too. The images in movies, in love songs, those hidden messages and innuendos, they spoke for Maggie. They sang for her now, too. Even if no one else sitting in history class knew it, which, of course, they didn't, Maggie had waged a private revolution and won.

"As soon as you have finished, you can give me your paper and you are free to go," Mr. Green, the history teacher, announced. Several kids stood up right away and filed toward the front of the room.

The girls' swim team was not boys' basketball or football or even lacrosse, so news of the impending championship was not spreading across the school like wildfire, nor was it on the tip of anyone's tongue, other than those of the girls themselves. But it had been announced over the loudspeaker in the morning, and some of the teachers followed girls' sports.

"Good work yesterday," Mr. Green said when Maggie dropped her paper on his desk. "You're going to the state semifinals, right?"

Maggie nodded.

"Well, you worked hard. You deserve this."

Maggie blushed, her cheeks warmed. "Thanks, Mr. Green."

Whatever Meghan Liggett had been so closely inspecting in the grass in front of her condo no longer seemed to hold her interest. When Leah dove into the pool, Meghan looked up.

"I think I am going to go down the slide now," Leah called out to Maggie. Loudly—she said it too loudly, and Maggie knew exactly what her sister was doing.

She wasn't sure which was making her more angry, her sister's naughty behavior—after Leah had just reprimanded Maggie and told her to sit on the stairs—or her apparent infatuation with the snobby neighbor girl.

Loudly, Maggie responded, "No, you're not, because Mommy won't let you."

Leah's head abruptly turned toward the lawns of the pool-facing condos. At exactly that moment, Meghan stood up and pretended to notice, for the first time, who had suddenly dived into the pool on this hot Saturday morning. Meghan's mouth formed a tiny O shape, and then, just as quickly, she appeared as indifferent as she could manage.

"Well, Mommy's not here. Is she?" Leah answered, nearly shouting at this point.

Maggie will remember the sun, which had been beating down on the identical red condo roofs, reflecting off the surface of the clean, aqua-blue pool water all morning, suddenly tuck itself behind a large cloud and stay there for what seemed like forever.

Fourteen

Five kids—two older brothers and two younger sisters, with Nathan smack in the middle—and for the most part, they all had similar personalities. Even with eight people at the table, it was quiet. No one seemed to feel they needed to be the center of attention. The older boys, Jeffrey (the one with the darker hair) and Thomas (the one with the tattoo on his wrist)—or maybe was it Jeffrey with the tattoo and Thomas with dark hair, as Maggie was having a hard time remembering which was which—hadn't said a word since they sat at the table.

"So, Maggie, you're on the swim team?" Nathan's mother asked.

"Yeah. We actually made it to the semifinals this year. They're in a couple of days."

"That's nice."

There was always something uncomfortable about eating at someone else's house. The food was a little unfamiliar and the way they set the table. Like how Julie's mother put out a wooden basket that held all the silverware and everyone reached over and grabbed what they needed. At her own house, her mother put out a folded paper napkin—always in a triangle—and nothing but a fork. If the meal required anything else, she would have to jump up and get one for everyone. Here, Nathan's mother used cloth napkins and every place had a fork, knife, and spoon, though Maggie couldn't figure out what she might need the spoon for. His mother had made baked ham, a string-bean casserole topped with dried onions, salad, and Pillsbury Crescent Rolls. And maybe there was going to be a dessert.

Maggie's family never served dessert. That was more of a fend-for-yourself, in-front-of-the-TV kind of thing: Oreos or Fig Newtons, if you could find them in the pantry.

But, despite what was different, it felt right sitting at this table. There was not only a sameness in disposition—gentle, if Maggie had to put a word to it—but in appearance. There was no denying that this was a family. The two younger sisters, Emily and Anne, were only eleven months apart. "Irish twins," Nathan's mother said when she introduced them, "but we're not Irish. It's just a saying.

"But I hear *you* have real twins in your family," she said to Maggie.

"Yeah, I have twin brothers. They're six."

Maggie tried to notice Nathan's face—he was sitting next to her—without being too obvious. She knew Nathan wouldn't like his mother cross-examining her, but she wondered if he had told her anything about Leah. Of course, what could he have said? Only what Maggie had told him.

"Do you have any sisters?" Anne (or possibly Emily) asked.

She was used to that question. If she answered, "I used to," it sounded provocative, like an invitation to more questions, or even glib, like a joke. The other person would be forced to ask what happened, as if maybe there were another explanation for "once" having a sister.

If she said, "I *did,* but my sister died," it was usually a big downer, as if she were trying to gain sympathy or, worse, garner unearned attention. But, somehow, to deny Leah's existence altogether felt wrong.

"Not anyone as annoying as you two," Nathan

131

answered. His tone was out of character enough to redirect Emily (or Anne) completely. For the next five minutes, Anne (or Emily), and then both of them, tried to convince Nathan that they were not annoying and never had been.

Leah

I was always able to convince my sister to give me all the best Easter candy out of her basket. We would both wake up early in the morning, Maggie's bed directly across the room from mine. And I had to be quick. Before our parents woke up.

"Let's dump it all on the floor and look at it," I would say.

Maggie was only two or three or four, and then five, so she would do it. She would do anything I asked her back then. She would do anything I did. She wanted to do everything I did. It was really annoying, to tell the truth, but sometimes I counted on it.

"Wow, look how much we have."

"Wow," Maggie repeated.

Spread out before us, between our two unmade beds, on the braided oval rug, were gooey marshmallow Peeps, eyes on and eyes hanging off; king-size peanut-butter eggs; *chocolate-covered coconut-cream eggs; miniature eggs covered in pink, yellow, and blue foil; flat brown bunnies disappointingly stamped on only one side; and tons of loose jelly beans that we had to pull one by one from the strings of colored plastic straw alive with static electricity. Each of us also had one large Easter bunny holding a basket himself, fully three-dimensional, still in its box, and visible through stiff cellophane — most likely hollow, but still the most coveted of the loot.*

"Let's put all our candy together," I suggested to Maggie. "We will have so much more that way."

I don't know if the illogic of this meant anything to my little sister or if she was just humoring me, acquiescing, if she really knew all along that I had nefarious motives, but I remember she would willingly push her mound of candy right into mine, with two baby hands, like a steam shovel.

"Wow," I would say.

"Wow."

The next step was easy. When I suggested we return our candy to our baskets before Mom and Dad woke up, I made sure that most of the chocolate eggs, the peanut-butter eggs, and the good-flavored jelly beans made their way into my basket. The yellow now eyeless Peeps, the green and red jelly beans, and the gross coconut-cream eggs landed back in hers. One year I tried to take both large packaged bunnies, but they didn't even fit, and I figured I would be blowing the whistle on myself.

But that last year, the very spring before I drowned, Maggie was old enough to know what was going on, or if she had known all along, she was finally old enough not to want to stand for it any longer.

"I don't want to put our candy together," she said.

"Shhh . . . not so loud."

"I still don't want to."

I sat on the floor, just as we always had, but something was different. I thought about reaching across our baskets and grabbing a chunk of her flesh, like right above her elbow, for instance, and squeezing really hard until she gave in, but instead I gave in. Maggie would give me any piece of candy I wanted anyway.

Sometimes, it was hard to tell what she added to my life and what she had taken away. I had been jealous since the day she was born, and I loved her more than anything I could think of. More than all the candy in the world.

I fished around in my basket until I felt one of those smooth, roundish foil-wrapped eggs, so delicious, pure chocolate, just the right amount to pop in your mouth and small enough so that there were plenty of them. Pink, I found a pink one. Maggie's favorite color that year.

"Here." I handed it to her.

She took it, tore off the wrapper, and it disappeared into her mouth. "I love you, too," she said. When she smiled at me, she had chocolate all over her teeth.

Fifteen

"I really do have to get to some sleep," Maggie said. "Early practice."

"I know." Nathan had let the engine idle, its subtle vibration rocking the car like a lullaby. He had driven her home after dinner.

Maggie touched the door handle and paused. "Nathan?"

"Yeah?"

Drops of wetness started to hit the windshield, tinging and then bouncing off.

"Is it snowing?" Maggie asked.

Nathan leaned forward to look deeper out the front window. "No, not yet. I think it's sleet. You'd better get inside. You don't want to get wet."

Maggie opened the car door.

Nathan stopped her. "But what were you going to ask me? What were you going to say?"

"People tell me things, true things. All the time.

And then they don't want anything to do with me."
She pulled the door shut again.

"Like who?"

"Like people, like strangers, people at school. It's like they let me see what's inside and then they hate me for it," Maggie said. "I don't want that to happen to us."

"It won't. It can't," Nathan said. "There isn't anything I haven't told you already. And I'm still here."

"OK." Maggie reached for the door handle again.

Nathan took her arm. "Wait. I have something to tell you, then." He took a breath. "I love you, Maggie. I know I love you."

She looked back at Nathan, his face splattered with the reflection of the ice on the surface of the windshield, like freckles, like tiny distortions.

"Do *you* love *me*?" he asked. "Remember, you can't lie." Nathan managed a tentative smile.

"No, it's *you* that can't lie." Maggie laughed.

"I didn't."

"I know," she said. She put her hand on the door handle again. The cold seeped through her gloves and into her skin and made her shiver. "I love you, too."

It was so easy. Not like in the movies, where the music swells, the guy stammers, and the girl gets all nervous. It was easy. It was the truth.

Sunday, the first real winter day of the year, Maggie's parents told her they were splitting up. It snowed hard that afternoon. Really, it had never stopped. Sleet from the day before had turned to snow and fallen all through the night. A blinding whiteness outside the living-room window, clinging to every branch and roof, an oddly beautiful backdrop. Dylan and Lucas had apparently already been told *something,* but not the same thing Mr. and Mrs. Paris were now telling Maggie.

"Daddy and I aren't going to stay married any-more," Mrs. Paris phrased it. Maggie wondered if any other expressions had been considered, and if so, why was this the winner?

Daddy and I aren't going to stay married anymore.

"It shouldn't be that big of a surprise to you, is it?" Mrs. Paris asked.

Maggie looked over at her dad. The only word Maggie could think of was *wizened.* His face looked *wizened.* Her next thought was the swim meet the next day. If the team won that meet, the state semifinals, and then the state finals, they would be invited to Nationals over midwinter break. Most everyone had a parent, or two, or entire families, planning their vacation around the meet. Which of her parents would go with Maggie? And then if only one of them was there, would everyone have to find out? What if neither of them came?

Would they hate each other so much that they could never be in the same room together ever again? Maggie actually laughed out loud.

"It's nervous laughter," Mrs. Paris told her husband, although he hadn't said anything.

And then oddly, or maybe not so oddly — maybe it was exactly perfectly self-destructive — while her parents' mouths were moving and words were coming out, Maggie had another thought, about Matthew James and about how he would be coming home soon: The memory of how badly he had treated her seemed to fit the moment, seemed to fit the crime, fit *some* crime, and that was all that mattered. It was snowing, midwinter break. College students got out mad early. Matthew would be back in town soon, and of course, the deed had been done. She was ready.

"It's not going to happen right away, Maggie," Mrs. Paris said. Her eyes were shot with red and her mouth was trembling, which wasn't fair. Which wasn't fair at all. She had no right to be crying.

"I'm going to stay until I find something close by," Mr. Paris said. "Certainly not before the end of the swim season."

"But none of this has anything to do with you, Maggie," Mrs. Paris said quickly. She glanced at her husband. "We just want you to know that."

Not that she had thought of that, but now that they mentioned it, Maggie crinkled her face. *Why would this have anything to do with me? How could this be my fault? Why would they say that?*

Mrs. Paris was standing, while Mr. Paris sat on the couch.

"Where's Dylan and Lucas?"

Maggie's parents looked at each other. "They're at Grandma's. Why?"

Maggie shrugged. She didn't have to say anything.

"We both love you very much, Maggie," Mrs. Paris said.

"Of course we do," Mr. Paris said. "This has nothing to do with you."

They said it again.

But Maggie had no way of knowing anymore

if they were telling the truth, if anyone ever had. It all seemed so ridiculous. And embarrassing. All Maggie knew was that she didn't want anyone to know. Not even Julie.

Sixteen

The girls' semifinal swim meet was a two-and-a-half-hour bus ride away, smack in the middle of the day. Only the particularly devoted, or crazed, parents could attend, like Mr. Paris. Over the rhythm of the seams in the highway and the steady sound of the motor, nothing was heard but the tiny thumping beats escaping from iPods and an occasional cough or sneeze. The intensity of the team's focus seemed to draw oxygen from the air.

What felt like seconds later, or years, Maggie found herself on the starting block, then she found herself in the water, and just like that it was all over. They were back on the bus, going home. They had won.

Maggie had sharp pains in her chest and belly on the ride home from the meet. She told Julie she thought she had an ulcer.

"Or maybe you're having a heart attack," Julie offered.

"Thanks."

The two friends sat low and close together, their knees wedged high against the back of the seat in front of them, their necks arched forward, pressed against the vinyl cushioning behind them.

"You swam great, Mags," Julie went on. "Maybe you just overdid it."

Maggie lifted her knees and slid her bottom back, sitting up. "I'm OK. Just hungry. When are we going to stop to eat? Did Coach say?"

And as if on cue, the air brakes hissed and the bus pulled into the rest stop. It was pitch-black outside, but the massive lights illuminating the parking lot made it look like it was noon.

"McDonald's!" A cheer rose.

"Health food, here we come!"

"Everybody has to give me their bonus points."

"Like hell."

"I'm getting two double cheeseburgers, and nobody can stop me."

And the girls piled off the bus with renewed energy.

"My treat," Coach Mac called out once they were inside. Winning makes everybody feel generous.

Standing in line, ordering, grabbing straws, pulling the toys out of Happy Meals, and finding a place to sit were all second nature. The girls spread out and were absorbed into the world of fast food, like children again. It was infectious—either the excitement, the bright lighting in the dark of night, or the smell of salty, warm French fries.

"My freakin' parents are such assholes." Cecily Keitel laid her tray down at the table and scooted into the bench seat across from Maggie. Julie was following right behind.

No encouragement needed, though Maggie was surprised Cecily was willing to talk so openly again. Repeat performances were rare.

"My freakin' dad wasn't even here. I broke my own record. Twice."

"I know. You swam great," Julie said. She unwrapped her burger and dumped her fries on a napkin. "Anybody want?"

"Are you kidding?" Maggie pointed to her own tray. She had two large fries and a large milk shake.

"Even *your* dad and mom were there," Cecily went on.

"What's that supposed to mean?" Julie asked,

but it was unusual for the Bensimons to come to a meet and stay the whole time.

"No offense," Cecily said. "Divorced parents suck. They hate each other so much that it leaks out all over the place, and then they try to talk to me about it. My mother keeps telling me how sorry she is."

"For what?" Maggie felt her stomach tighten again. She pushed her tray away.

"For anything. For everything that's happened in the last fifteen years. For my toilet training. For 9/11. For the recession. For the war in Iraq."

The three girls giggled. Maggie was too nervous to look at the other two for fear of spitting food out of her mouth.

"She's so damned sorry that I start to feel like it *is* my fault." Cecily was on a roll.

"Maybe it is," Maggie blurted out. It was as if all the power had suddenly been drained from her body, as if a counterclockwise rotation stopped, reversed, and started to spin in the other direction.

Julie coughed, then began choking.

Cecily smacked Julie on the back and glared at Maggie. "What?"

"What?" Julie echoed.

"I don't mean *you*. I mean *me*. I mean, my parents are getting divorced. They told me last night. It sucks. It just sucks." The release itself was like one pain replacing another, creating relief in its place.

Neither Julie nor Cecily spoke. There was that beat or two when Maggie might still burst out laughing and tell everyone at the table that she had been joking.

Maggie went on, "So now I'm thinking my dad is going to move away. Or are they going to have to sell the house? And does he have to give my mother money now? All they do is fight about money."

Julie was quiet. Her expression went from hurt to compassionate. "You didn't tell me."

"It just happened," Maggie explained. "Last night. I feel sick to my stomach. I feel like it's my fault."

"I hate to break this to you, Maggie," Cecily said. She lifted her soda. "No matter what you think, you're just not that powerful."

"You OK, Maggie?" Julie's voice melted into dark.

The bus moved into the darkness, deeper into the night. Most of the girls had fallen asleep.

"Yeah, I guess so."

"Everything's going to be OK," Julie said.

"I don't know. Now I'm the one confessing things to perfect strangers. I've lost my mojo."

"Well, Cecily's not exactly a stranger. And it's not like you were so happy about hearing everybody's bitching and moaning."

"Well, better them than me."

Julie said, "But you could have told me. I'm your best friend."

"You are," Maggie whispered back. "I'm sorry."

"It's OK."

Someone's cell phone vibrated insistently.

Lucid dreaming is really nothing more than being aware that you are dreaming while you are dreaming. In other words, you know it isn't real and that you are asleep and dreaming. Sometimes, when she was particularly exhausted, Maggie drifted into REM sleep almost immediately, or maybe that night it was the food she ate for dinner, too many French fries, a bite of Cecily's apple pie, that last slurp of vanilla milk shake.

But this certainly was a dream, because Leah was dead and she could not be talking, but she was. Even Leah seemed to know she was not alive. Maggie wanted to tell her about their parents, about

145

what was happening. Every time she opened her mouth, it was flooded with water, but Maggie could speak anyway.

Leah, I have to tell you something, but don't be mad. Don't be mad at me.

Each word rose in a bubble to the surface. Leah wasn't listening. Why wouldn't she listen? She had been under the water so long, and yet she seemed OK.

Except you need gills to breath underwater.

Or a blowhole. A dolphin swam by with Leah on her back, too fast. She was swimming too fast to hear what Maggie had to say.

I have to wake up.

I need to wake up.

This is an awful dream, and I want to wake up.

Now.

Now.

Maggie woke and sat up in bed. Her bedroom door flew open, and both her mother and father stood in the light.

"What's wrong? What's the matter? You were crying in your sleep."

Maggie didn't register why her dad was

standing there, too; she was just so glad he was home. Everything was going to be all right.

"Everything's OK now, sweetie," he said.

Her mother asked, "Why are you still crying?"

"I'm not," Maggie said, but when she reached her hand to her cheek, she felt that her face was dripping. Then she realized that her blankets were soaked and that a small pool of water had formed around the bed.

It wasn't until she woke up again, her eyes wet, that Maggie realized she had still been dreaming.

Seventeen

"Look, don't say anything about my parents, OK?"

"I would never do that," Julie said.

Luckily, there was an assembly first period. Maggie felt drained and tired. She hadn't slept well. She'd texted Nathan late, telling him she was home and that they had won the meet, but she didn't say anything about her parents.

"Just promise," Maggie said to her friend. "Not even to Nathan."

"Promise."

They walked down the hall. It felt empty, with most of the seniors blowing off the assembly.

"Wait for me." Nathan sprang up behind them. He grabbed Maggie by the waist.

"So what's this assembly about, anyway?" Julie's voice sounded funny, but Nathan didn't notice. She always had a hard time keeping a secret.

"Character building," Nathan told her. "He's supposed to be funny. That's all I heard."

As they neared the auditorium, they could hear the crowd jostling and settling inside. The teachers were directing everyone where to sit and to be quiet, waving their arms and looking generally annoyed. The phys ed teacher was telling kids to put away their soda bottles. No food allowed in the auditorium. The vice principal was already escorting two boys out the far-left doors. The back and side seats were pretty much taken.

"C'mon." Julie took Maggie's hand. Nathan followed in a chain. "Let's go up front."

It was the last week before midwinter vacation, and there was already a buzz in the air. Not much work left to be done. No one wanted work over the break. There was a percentage of the student body that had already left, taking the extra two days, against school policy and despite repeated warnings that had come home in flyers and e-mails to parents.

Nathan, Maggie, and Julie shifted in their seats, three rows from stage center, just as the principal, Mr. Walker, walked across and stood before the microphone. There was the usual tech malfunction before a loud screech and then Mr. Walker's voice: "We'd like to welcome Hans Butcher to our school this morning." He lifted his hand toward stage right.

Mr. Walker was still talking, but the audience seemed to think they were being cued to clap.

When it was quiet again, the principal continued. "Hans is engaging, entertaining, and affecting. He will challenge us all to take responsibility for ourselves and our actions."

Mr. Walker took a piece of folded paper from his pocket and finished up by reading. "As a youth, Hans struggled with both a learning disability and a complete lack of direction. After struggling to graduate from high school, Hans spent the next few years with no ambition. His life changed when he finally understood that it wasn't his learning disabilities, or any other outside factor, holding him back in life. It was only his self-limiting beliefs and the labels he had placed on himself and allowed others to place on him."

The rest of the speech went on to describe Hans's great achievements and how he would unlock the hidden potential within us all. Three kids were already fast asleep, but they woke up briefly when the clapping began again and Hans Butcher appeared on the stage and took the microphone.

He *was* funny. He was loud and energetic. He moved back and forth, using the entire space. Hans told his life story and did magic tricks in between, while making rapid-fire jokes. Still, four kids near the back were now asleep.

"And now, ladies and gentlemen," Hans announced, standing with his arms at his sides, palms out, as if in complete surrender, "comes the hypnotism portion of the show. I am going to prove that every one of you here, sitting in this audience, is a liar. And that only I can compel you to tell the truth."

Maggie felt her whole body tense, on alert. Her heart quickened, and when she looked over at Julie, she could see that her friend was having a similar reaction.

"What does he mean?" Julie said, leaning over.

Maggie whispered, "I don't know."

"Do I have any volunteers?" Hans Butcher said.

About two dozen hands went up, but Hans ignored them. "I am looking for someone specific," he said, "someone with a secret."

Hands continued to wave around in the air, as well as jeers about particular football players, cheerleaders, and a few teachers. In the anonymity of the auditorium, all was fair.

"Don't worry, Mr. Pierson—we already know you're gay."

"C'mon, Stewart, get up there and tell them about you and your mama."

"Don't worry, Melissa—he's not talking about last night."

Then, as if he were expecting things to get out of control exactly as they did, Hans Butcher calmed his audience by doing nothing more than speaking more softly and raising his hand as if he were about to pick someone. "The person I am looking for is mostly quiet and shy, a loner, in fact, although by choice. If provoked, this person will make things happen precisely as they need them to."

Nathan clucked his tongue. "He's using contradictory descriptions that can fit everyone. He's a con man."

But Maggie couldn't take her eyes off the stage and the man who was parading around, calling out words, accusing and seducing. She felt cold, and her spine involuntarily compressed then released in a shudder.

Hans said, "How about you, young man?"

One of the jeering football players stood up. "Sure."

New hands shot up.

"And how about you? And this pretty girl?" Hans proceeded to pick three more students and one teacher—a "good sport"—from their seats. Meanwhile, someone had walked onstage and set up five metal folding chairs. Without being told, the volunteers took their seats, facing forward, all in a row.

Hans Butcher went through a series of relaxation exercises. He waved his hands a lot. He talked fast. He talked slowly, and sure enough, one by one, each of the five began to lower their eyelids and then nod their heads until they all appeared to be sleeping.

"No one really tells the truth. Not to themselves in particular," Hans Butcher said, his subjects all resting comfortably, or as comfortably as one could be sitting up onstage in a metal folding chair. "On any given day, the average person tells seven to ten minor lies." He paused dramatically. "And one to two major ones."

The audience had gotten very quiet. It seemed to Maggie the lights had been lowered.

"Now, when I snap my fingers, any one of you"—he addressed the five—"who is holding a minor secret, something benign, something you wouldn't be afraid to tell two hundred of your closest friends"—the audience laughed nervously—"please feel free to tell us now."

One girl, center stage, number three in the middle seat, stood up immediately. Lots of heads swiveled around, then turned back to the stage. The girl was a senior. Her name, when Hans prompted her to speak, was Louisa.

"Louisa," Hans began, "I don't want you to tell us anything you will regret later on. Are you sure you want to tell us?"

Louisa nodded in a kind of drunken stupor.

Louisa began to speak, her eyes still half closed. "I was at a party last night—"

Hans interrupted her again. "Please do not name any other names, understood?"

Onstage, Louisa nodded again. "Everyone was drinking."

"Wow, some secret that is," a male voice shouted

from the darkened house seats, but Hans paid no attention and no one else on the stage even seemed to hear.

"No parents were home." The audience groaned. "So no one was really paying attention to the house—just to each other. The boys all wanted to find someone to have sex with, and the girls pretended not to care if no one wanted to have sex with them."

"This is a setup," Nathan whispered. There were other uncomfortable comments floating around the audience.

"And this house was really rich. I mean, the people who live there are really rich. Like rock-star rich. I started to hate them." Louisa still spoke in a monotone, seeming not to know where she was or to whom she was talking.

"And why did you hate these people? They weren't even home, am I correct?" Hans prompted her.

Louisa nodded. "I didn't hate them. I hated that they had what I didn't have."

"Which was what?"

"Nice things," Louisa said, her voice more animated now. "Stuff. So I wanted to take something. Something no one would miss."

Hans suddenly snapped his fingers, and Louisa's eyes flew open. She seemed to have no idea what had just transpired. She looked to the other four subjects and then out to the audience with a bewildered expression on her face.

"There is the voice we all have in our heads," Hans went on, "the voice that perpetuates the narrative of our lives. It talks and talks, noticing the world, deciding what we will do or won't do. Expressing our anger and our sadness and our frustrations. Noticing that pretty girl. That hot guy. It knows the answers to the test. Or not."

More laughter.

"But there is another voice we don't often listen to. It's quieter," Hans said. "You can't hear it while the other voice is talking."

Hans went on to do the same hypnotic act with the remaining volunteers, stopping each before he or she had gone too far. Each time, Hans used the confession as an opportunity to talk about taking responsibility. Being a better person. Tolerance. He was earning his PTO check at his subjects' expense.

"*He* stole your mojo," Julie said as they filed out with the crowd toward the rows of double doors.

The light in the lobby was stark. It felt like hours had gone by.

"Well, at least I know where it went," Maggie said. She forced a laugh.

Nathan reached back and held out his hand, but Maggie pulled away, subtly enough that it seemed accidental. A motion so deft that even Maggie would look back and wonder if it had happened or not. She would wonder if everything that happened before and everything that happened after had ever been in her control at all.

Leah

Sometimes when I'm sleeping, Maggie comes over to my bed and watches me. I know she does this, even though I keep my eyes shut tight, and I am very good at not moving. I don't move an inch. If I am perfectly still, I think she will go away, go back to her own bed. Sometimes Maggie can't sleep at night and wants to come into bed with me.

She knows as much as I do that she could just go into Mom and Dad's room. They would grunt sleepily and shift over and let her right under their covers, but she wants me. She wants to see if I'm awake, too, because she doesn't want me to be mad at her for bothering me. "Don't bother me. You always bother me," *I'd say.*

And I know that hurts her feelings, and I also know she doesn't care. She knows she isn't really bothering me. I mean, she is, but I'm used to it.

But tonight I will roll over and I will make room for Maggie to climb into bed right next to me. She needs me now.

Eighteen

There would be an easy practice tomorrow, right before the finals, but today would be brutal. No letting up on anyone.

"Do people really say you don't sweat in the water?" Maggie said. She held on to the side of the pool and tried to calm her chest heaving.

Julie held on beside her. "Is my face as red as it feels?"

"Redder. You look like a cherry. You match your cap."

Coach Mac was standing on the bulkhead, leaning in, gesturing in all sorts of wild ways. The 200-meter relay needed to work on their turning technique. Any second the assistant coach was going to stroll over and give the girls their next set of drills.

157

"I'm not feeling so good, Jules," Maggie said. "Can you cover for me?"

"Cover for you? How?"

"Jules, I can't breathe. I can't catch my breath."

The assistant coach was still filling in papers on a clipboard while Coach Mac was repeating his flip-turn pantomime, over and over.

"OK, just go," Julie said.

Maggie put her hands on the deck and hoisted her body out of the water. It never stopped amazing her how light her body felt in the water. If she could be that weightless on dry land, she would fly.

She wanted to fly.

Maggie sat down on a bench in the locker room. She put her hand to her heart to calm its beating and relieve the tightness constricting the flow of air. She counted to ten, then fifteen, and slowly the burning lessened, and then slowly it stopped altogether. Back on the pool deck, she moved along the wall, trying to blend in with the grayness and slip back into the water.

"I told the coach you had to go to the bathroom," Julie said to her when Coach Mac gave the girls a short break. "You OK now?"

"Yeah, I'm fine," Maggie said, "but everyone knows we all pee in the pool."

Julie smiled. "Don't get me started."

The whistle blew; their break was over.

Maggie didn't think that what her sister was doing was swimming—not real swimming anyway, even if it had gotten her a deep-water pass at camp last summer. It looked to Maggie like the doggie paddle as Leah headed right out to the middle of the pool.

She could have shouted out, reminded Leah about how soon Mommy was coming home. Made fun of her stroke. Stopped her. Called her back. Told her she wasn't going to be able to hide her wet hair.

Stopped her. She could have stopped her.

Leah didn't say anything while she made her way toward the slide and the ladder on the other side. Her head was barely above the water. Maggie remembers her sister's head looking like a funny insect skimming the surface, bobbing up and down, like those water bugs you see on ponds and streams. When she got to the other side, Leah held on and waved back at Maggie.

"Hey there, Sis," she called out.

Leah never called her that. It was all for Meghan's benefit, to sound cool. To look like a big shot.

Maggie looked over to see if Meghan was outside,

still acting as if she didn't notice anyone in the blue, blue pool—to see if Meghan was still standing on her green, green lawn—but she had gone.

Things at home were so strangely the same that Maggie was able to ignore the surreal conversation she had had with her parents about divorce. The tension was still there, in the short responses and averted eyes, but if anything, her parents were fighting a little less. It was easy to pretend it hadn't happened and that it wouldn't happen, like a bad dream you can't quite remember.

The morning of the state finals, Maggie woke up before her alarm went off, before any of the three fail-safe clocks—her cell phone, desk clock, and computer—chimed. The blackness always confused her. Was it morning? Was it midnight? Was it only a few minutes after she had fallen asleep or hours later? Finally she just got out of bed and flipped on the light in the bathroom. Only then did she remember her dreams. It was sometimes hard to distinguish a memory from a dream. Had that really happened, or had she dreamed it?

The house was silent. It was four thirty, December dark. Too late to go back to sleep. She had to get up in twenty minutes anyway.

Hosting the state finals was big business for West Hill. The athletic director, Mr. Eli, who had never come to a meet before, was wandering around checking on the ticket booth, the raffle booth, the two separate concessions. Six schools were all converging for a ten-hour event. Hundreds of spectators, competitors, and coaches. There were even rumors of scouts from Florida State, Penn State, and the University of Maryland being there.

"I didn't think I'd find you here," Nathan said. "I looked everywhere."

Maggie was crouched by the entrance to the old boys' locker room. It wasn't used much, and the whole wing was slated to be torn down, renovated for a new ceramics and woodworking shop, but the water was still turned on. The sinks ran, the toilets flushed.

"Are you nervous?"

Maggie nodded. She was wearing her flannel pajama pants, a sweatshirt, and her pool sandals. Her goggles bulged from the side of her suit where they were stuffed into the leg opening. Her cap was bunched up in her fist.

"Are my parents here?" Maggie asked. "I haven't seen my dad yet. Is my dad here?" She had scanned the bleachers when she came in but hadn't seen her father.

"I don't know. I didn't see him, but it's mobbed out there. I could tell you it's just a swim meet, right?" Nathan tried.

She nodded again.

"But that would be stupid, right?"

Nathan sat down beside Maggie. "Or that it's supposed to be fun?" he tried.

"It's not," Maggie said. "Listen, I've been thinking about something. I wanna make a date."

"A date?"

"For ten years from now," Maggie went on.

"What?"

"I don't mean a date date, like a going out on a date. But a real number, a calendar date. For us to meet in the future, in our futures."

Nathan shifted back. "Huh?"

Maggie pulled at Nathan's arm. "Just wait. Just do this for me. Ten years from now, we meet at the Dutch Reformed church on Old Main Street. OK? Say, like, twelve noon. So wherever we are, whatever we're doing, in ten years we each make it there at the exact same time, OK? No matter what?"

"And what if we're still together? Did you even consider that?"

"Yeah, I did. If we're still together, then we just have an anniversary. We go out to dinner or something. We mark ten years from when we first . . . you know."

"You know the date?"

"You don't know that date?"

"Yeah, I know it."

"OK, so ten years from that exact day. You can't forget. I'll write it down for us both, and you have to put it in a safe place. No matter what happens, we have to be there."

Nathan stood up. "You must be really nervous, Maggie. It's just a swim meet. If you guys lose, at least you can sleep in the rest of the semester. We can actually go to the movies."

Maggie got to her feet beside him. "No, promise, Nathan. Promise me you'll be there."

"And eat pizza in public."

"I'm serious. Will you be there? No matter what?"

"OK. OK," Nathan said. "I promise."

Her knees were shaking so much, it would have been audible in a silent room, the knocking together of her bones. Maggie knew that *real* athletes lived for these moments, for the moments when the difference between winning and losing hung in the balance, in determination, in flesh and muscles. And this moment was far from silent. There was cheering and yelling from the stands and the deck, and the echo of stomping on the metal risers was deafening. Then, just before the referee lifted the whistle to his mouth, the sounds lowered to an unnatural stillness. Maggie's body seemed to know what to do, even if she didn't. Her grip, the arch of her back, the readiness of her shoulders.

"Swimmers on your marks. Get set. Go."

So many times Maggie had wondered about all the tiny things that might have been different. One shift in the lineal sequence of events, in somebody's decision, one choice, no matter how irrelevant, and the story changes completely. Maggie was the only one who saw Leah's considerable feat of both courage and skill. Maybe if she had looked impressed, if she had clapped.

Maybe if Meghan had come back out or stayed to see it the first time.

Instead, Maggie watched her sister head out again, across the pool, across the deep water. By this time, Maggie was getting anxious. She kept turning her gaze from the water to the road, where she thought she might see her mother's car returning.

But there were so many silver cars. Which one was her mom's? She didn't know, but at some point, her fear of being caught outside the apartment had changed to the hope that her mother would get back and find them, even if it meant getting in *big trouble*.

Maggie stood on the concrete deck now, taking a tiny step forward, another one back, her footprints drying in the heat almost as quickly she shifted from leg to leg. The last thing she remembers is the sun all of a sudden bursting out from behind the cloud where it had been hidden. She remembers thinking it was funny, as if someone had just flipped on a light switch.

But oh, no, they were outside. That's funny.

The sunlight created a glare, a blinding reflection on the surface of the pool, so that everything became invisible, a white burst of blur. Maggie put her hand to her forehead to create a brim of shade, and when she was able to see again, she couldn't see her sister anymore.

When a swimmer is right on your shoulder and you can hear her breathing, her strokes pulling and gliding, the splash of her hand slapping the water, her velocity and mass creating a momentum you cannot deny, it is all a blur. Everything you know about swimming flies away, and all you can do is hold your breath until your lungs are about to burst, until the pain is so great, and then push on past it.

You don't see anything, not the line on the bottom of the pool, not your own hands diving through the surface and grabbing the water as if it were lead and forcing it behind you. You don't see the marker, the end, the electronic timer pressed up against the side. You reach past it, beyond it. You swim as if you are going to crash right into the wall and never stop swimming.

Maggie hit the touch pad. Her head lifted into the air, and her lungs involuntarily filled with oxygen. A millisecond sooner and they would have taken in water, because that's what lungs do. They breathe.

The LCD scoreboard lit up instantly with all the finishing times. All heads turned to look. Maggie's lane recorded 4:12.41. In lane 5, right next to hers, the numbers read 4:12.02. Maggie had lost by less than four tenths of a second, an amount of time no human brain could comprehend. If she were swimming prior to 1912, the race would have been determined by a judge. He might have called a tie or made his decision based on bias. He might have blinked.

He might have lied because he would have been human. Maggie didn't think of any of these things. The team had lost their chance of going to Nationals.

The definition of time is, itself, circular. The very quantity needed to explain time is time itself. It relies on the acceptance that time is linear, made up of events in sequence, and time is the interval between them. Theoretically, in a dreamlike state, there is an infinite measure of the space from beginning to end. It never stops.

In three days, the high school would be on midwinter break, a quarter of the kids would get on a plane to some Caribbean island. In eleven hours and fourteen minutes, the sun would rise again and it would be tomorrow. In five days—in 120 hours, in 7,200 minutes—it would be the shortest day of the year, the winter solstice, and sometime after that, Matthew James would be returning home from college. Or so said his Facebook update, which Maggie hadn't looked at in more than two weeks, or fifteen days, a perfectly reasonable amount of time.

"Dad? Mom?" she called out. "Dylan?" Maggie realized she sounded weak. It was hard for her to get enough force behind her voice. "Lucas?" she called out, louder, but no one responded. Mrs. Paris appeared instead, at the top of the stairs. She didn't move to come down.

"Who dropped you off?"

"Julie's mom. Where were you guys? Where are Dylan and Lucas?"

"They're at Grandma's."

"Again?" Maggie asked.

"Yes."

"Where's Dad?" Maggie asked, but she already knew. She knew now why he wasn't at the meet. Why he wasn't home.

The dress coat, the one he never wore, the one that hung year after year on the same hook in the hall, was no longer there. She looked down to the spot where his old sneakers were supposed to be sitting, side by side, worn only on weekends to jog. Without a word, Maggie ran upstairs, past her mother, and flung open the door to her father's office. Mr. Paris didn't often work at home, but he kept all his papers, his computer—her dad wouldn't go anywhere without his computer—his books, letters he hadn't opened, on a wooden table in an extra room on the second floor.

The table was gone. Papers, stacked or boxed, sat on the floor, pushed into one corner. No computer anywhere to be seen.

"You lied!" Maggie yelled. "You lied to me. He left. He said he'd stay, but he's gone."

Mrs. Paris had come, almost, into the room by now. She stood leaning on the door frame, her arms crossed over her chest.

"What are you talking about? Nobody lied. We both told you. We sat down together and talked to you about this." Her voice was shaking. "Why are you crying, Maggie? You knew about this."

"I'm not crying," Maggie said, because she wasn't and wouldn't.

"You disappoint me. How are Lucas and Dylan going to be able to handle this if you can't?"

There was a familiar voice in Maggie's head, talking to her. And now it was angry. It repeated Mrs. Paris's words, each one, just to make sure Maggie understood, and then filed them away for future use. In an instant, the voice tried out a shocking response and gave its approval.

"I disappoint *you*," Maggie shouted back. "Are you fucking serious?"

She had never cursed at her mother before, but if any occasion seemed to call for it—and seemed likely to go unpunished—this was it.

Mrs. Paris took a deep breath. Her chest heaved up and down, taking her arms with it. Finally she spoke again. "We didn't lie to you. Your father moved out this morning. He — *we* thought it would be easier if you kids didn't have to watch."

"Really?"

"Yes, really. Believe it or not, we were thinking of what would be best for you and the boys."

Did her mother truly believe that her life, the way she behaved, the choices she made, had ever been for anyone other than herself?

"Like the way you left me and Leah alone?"

Maggie could see her mother's body start to tremble. She watched as her mother's face melted into another form, older, more tired. It was still her mother, but it wasn't.

"I left to buy food. I left you safe inside the house. I told you to stay inside." Mrs. Paris's voice was unnaturally pitched, and with each word, it got higher, louder, and less familiar. "And why don't you ask where your father was that day? It was Saturday, wasn't it? Where was your father? Why don't you ever ask that?"

Too late, Mrs. Paris's hand flew up to her mouth and locked, a riveted metal clamp.

Maggie figured that her sister had gotten out of the water.

Boy, she is fast.

Maggie kept her hand like a hat over her eyes and scanned the concrete that surrounded the pool. There would be footprints, wouldn't there? Little wet Leah footprints. *She wouldn't just leave me like this, would she?*

The sun was so hot, but water couldn't dry that fast. It had been a second, less than a second, since she had turned to look for Meghan. And Maggie was pretty sure there were no footprints. Leah shot up out of the water, just her face, her eyes wider than Maggie had ever seen them. No voice came out of her mouth, just a fierce popping sound.

Maggie would never, as long as she lived, forget that sound. It was not the sound of human gasping, not a feral, wordless cry for help, but the actual rush of air forcing its way into Leah's lungs. Pop.

Maggie could finally breath again. Mrs. Paris was completely defeated, but Maggie took in huge gulps of air and felt energized, alive. Mrs. Paris's whole person fell slack, as if she had no control over her own body. Her arms fell to her sides. Her entire weight was slumped against the door frame. If you took away the house, she would fall over completely.

She was ugly, old and ugly. Maggie didn't want to look at her anymore. Ever again.

Anger was joy and freedom. Maggie raced to her room and slammed the door behind her, the echo unnaturally loud. There were no locks—the house was old and the doors were fitted with wrought-iron bars and latches—but long ago Maggie had learned that shoving a hair barrette into the space just above the bar would prevent the latch from being lifted and, in effect, lock her bedroom door.

Maggie stood on her side of the door and waited for her mother's footsteps. She listened to hear her mother stomp up the stairs, stop in front of her door, maybe jiggle at the handle, but there were no such sounds. The house was quiet. All Maggie could hear was her own heart pumping with oxygen. Adrenaline whooshed through her arms and legs, every vein and muscle. It was deafening.

Maggie flipped on her CD player. She didn't recognize the music, but that didn't matter. It filled the space. She twisted the dial loud enough to obliterate everything else. She stood in the center of her room, which had once been a play stage for singing, for make-believe and pretending, a place of dreams, which now seemed broken. The wholeness of it all, the math. Two becomes four becomes three becomes five becomes four again. Why was this happening to her? She had lost her race and let down the team. Her sister was gone, her dad. It was all her fault.

Maggie looked in the mirror that hung over her bureau. Bad is ugly.

Maggie wasn't speaking, but the lips of the girl in the mirror were moving. The angry voice was talking, but Maggie didn't understand the language. She leaned closer to listen.

What are you saying?

It was a face she knew better than her own, the eyes and mouth and chin, the pores of skin, the follicles of hair, and the dark hair. A young face. A face to kiss, and pinch, and get angry at, with a mouth that eats ice cream and Easter candy, and the unwanted vegetables from Maggie's plate when no one is watching. She hated that face; she loved that face.

Listen.

What is she saying?

And then her cell phone chimed, a text: *Yo baby. I'm home early from SUNY. Wanna hang?*

Matthew suggested she meet him just down the block and around the corner from her house, where apparently he was texting her from. Maggie invented a story as she cut across her neighbor's lawn: Matthew had a fight with his girlfriend; she drove away crying. Matthew was upset at having hurt her but was now free. His first thoughts were of Maggie.

Her toes were frozen, but sweat dripped down her back. Maggie imagined her face was blotchy and red from the wind and the walk. She hadn't seen her mother on the way out, but she had left the music blasting in her room, set to repeat.

"Hey there," Matthew said. He rolled down the window of his car. "C'mon. It's cold out there."

Maggie walked around, opened the passenger side, and dropped into the front seat. Inside, heat poured from the vents, and the radio was broadcasting the end of a college basketball game.

"Damn." Matthew slammed his fist on the dashboard. "Oh, well. They suck."

Matthew turned to Maggie and said nothing. Instead, he grasped the back of her head and forced his tongue deep inside her mouth. He tasted forceful and unapologetic. Maggie could feel herself leaving her body. Being there but not being there.

"I don't have much time," Matthew told her, and

Maggie wondered what he did with his time. She knew nothing about him, which meant she had no reason to feel bad that he knew nothing about her. Matthew pushed his hand inside Maggie's coat, squeezed her left breast, and groaned. "Let's go somewhere more private."

Matthew shifted into drive.

Somewhere more private—though Maggie had never actually agreed—turned out to be the back of the Fairway shopping center. Most of the stores, other than Friendly's, were closed. The old video store had been empty for five years. The dry cleaner's had locked up and left for the day. No one went to the Variety Newsstand and Convenience Store anyway. Its shelves were always empty. Mr. Paris used to joke that it was probably a front for some terrorist organization, which no one else thought was particularly funny. But in any case, the back lot had only three scattered parked cars. Matthew took the farthest spot, near the woods and the chain-link fencing. He left the car running.

Why talk? Maggie didn't have anything to say— but she knew she could provide what Matthew had been wanting. She was an expert now. A real woman in control of herself—her present and her future, if not the past. She held the greatest power, which, at that moment, meant having no power at all.

When he entered her, Maggie closed her eyes as her body blew into a million pieces and dispersed, like feathers in the wind, oil into water, light into darkness.

Maggie opened her eyes again, straining to see Leah's face as it seemed to float just above the surface of the water.

"Leah?" Maggie tried to read the look on her sister's face. "Are you OK?"

There was nothing in her mind that could speak to what was happening. If Leah was hurt or needed her, she would call out, as she had when she fell off her bike last week, when blood had formed at the surface of Leah's knee and on the palms of her hands.

"Get help, you dummy! Go get Mommy!" Leah had yelled that day.

But then again, there was the time Leah had tripped holding a glass bottle filled with flowers while she ran across the backyard. The bottle shattered and cut right through Leah's thin T-shirt, but Maggie was ordered not to say anything.

"Don't you dare tell Mommy. You hear me? Don't ever tell her."

Now Leah was silent. Her eyes were like an owl's, perfectly round, pleading, maybe, but Maggie didn't know what they were saying. And then Leah went under the water again, so Maggie stepped closer to the edge of the pool. She walked around the perimeter, toward the deep end, where Leah had just disappeared.

"Leah?" Maggie called out again. "Are you OK?"

Matthew dropped Maggie off at her house. When she opened the door, she noticed that the music had stopped and her dad's running shoes were still missing.

"Mom?" she called out. "Mom?"

"Maggie?" It was her father.

"Dad."

Mr. Paris was sitting at the kitchen table with a mug of coffee cupped in his hands, as if he had never left.

"You don't look so good, sweetie. What's wrong?"

"Nothing. What are you doing here? I thought you moved out." Maggie said it as if maybe it weren't true. "You left. You don't belong here anymore."

Like a little kid, stomping her foot, throwing a tantrum, and hoping someone will stop her and make all the bad feelings go away, because she can't. She doesn't know how.

"I know," Mr. Paris said. Guilt sure does weaken a person. He would never have tolerated her talking to him this way before. "Your mother called me and said you were very upset, and then she said you ran away."

"I didn't run away." The memory of what had just happened burned between her thighs, and shame burned her face.

"Well, she thought you did. Are you OK?"

Long ago—long, long ago—Maggie would fall asleep on pretty much any car ride her family took, whether an hour and a half or ten minutes. It was kind of a joke in their family that Maggie would be asleep before their dad shifted the car into drive. And if it was late at night when they pulled up to the house, Maggie would try to remain as still as she could so that her dad would have to lift her little body out of the car and carry her into the house.

As she stood there now, Maggie remembered the amazing feeling of being in her dad's strong arms. She thought about how the world sounded, passing around her—the voice of her sister complaining that she could walk perfectly well on her own, her mother's high heels clicking on the kitchen floor, the lights being flipped on—and all the while she rode high above it, as if she were flying.

And she started to cry.

"Maggie, talk to me," Mr. Paris said. "Your mother told me what she said. She didn't mean that. Nobody blames you for what happened. You weren't even there. We know that."

Where were you, Dad? It was a Saturday. Where were you?

Leah's head came up to the surface one more time, but only for a moment. She no longer looked panicked. She looked calm. She looked peaceful.

When Leah slipped underwater again, a single ripple appeared on the surface of the water. Maggie watched as the tiny wave spread wider and wider, until it reached the edge of the pool. *Everything's going to be OK now. No need to bother the strangers sitting around the pool,* Maggie thought, and then she ran home.

She ran back to the apartment, but not before she took one look toward Meghan's front yard, and she thought she saw the front door closing. She should run there. It was closer. Ask Meghan for help. Maybe Meghan's mother was home, inside, cooking or cleaning, like mommies do. And weren't there other people around the pool? There was a couple of old grandparents, playing cards. They looked annoyed. They hadn't looked up once. The boy and the girl, kissing on the grass. Maybe they could help. But when Maggie turned to where she had seen them, they were no longer there.

Nothing was OK. Nothing was ever going to be OK again, and somehow Maggie knew it.

She just didn't know what to do.

Daddy. I need to get Daddy. Daddy will know what to do.

They had left the house unlocked, so Maggie was able to squeeze the handle, push open the door, and slip inside. It was hot, still so hot without the air-conditioning. She took in as much as she could, widening her eyelids and actually sucking in the light. Were there groceries on the counter? Were Daddy's keys hanging by the front door? Was the TV on in the kitchen? Because Mommy liked to watch her talk shows while she was putting the food away.

It would be best to approach this problem carefully. She didn't want to get her sister in trouble.

Leah hated that. Leah hated it when Maggie told on her.

"Never tattle," Leah had told her. "No one likes a tattletale."

Maggie looked up at the blue clock hanging above the sink. It had a picture of a fairy sitting on a rock, leaning forward and gazing into the water. The tiniest hand of the clock ticked with every second in a single jerking motion.

Leah.

Something told Maggie that time mattered. Time was loudly passing by, so she decided to just shout and let worry enter her voice. "Mommy? Daddy? Are you home?"

How much time went by? Maggie ran upstairs and downstairs, and finally she ran outside again, and when she got back, to Leah, to the fence that surrounded the pool, there was all kinds of noise, sirens and shouting. There were lights, and people, so many people. Where had they come from? How much time had passed? There had been no one a minute ago, and now there were hundreds and hundreds and thousands of people. And there was Mommy, crying.

Leah

I was three and a half years old when my little sister, Magdalena, was born. Her name was supposed to be Gwendolyn. At least, that's what my mother told me when she and my dad left for the hospital. They came back the next day; my mother was holding the baby. I couldn't see anything because she was so tiny, wrapped in a blanket like a Hot Pocket.

"Here's little baby Maggie," *my mother said. She bent down a little, even though it looked like it hurt her to do that.*

"Baby Gwen," *I corrected her.* How could a mother forget her own baby's name? *I was thinking.* This isn't a good sign, right off the bat.

"Baby Maggie," *my mother said.* "We decided in the hospital when we saw her. She's a Maggie, for sure."

But you can't just do that. You can't just change your baby's name whenever you feel like it. I felt a panic in my stomach, like when I eat too much candy. What if they decided to change my name? Who would I be?

"Baby Gwen," *I said again.* They just had to see the light.

My dad was hiding behind the video camera, and I could see him shaking with laughter. He was filming us, me and my new sister. This was one of those big moments, like my third birthday party. Like Christmas morning.

"No, sweetie. It's Maggie. We named her Maggie," my dad was saying.

They clearly thought this was the funniest thing that had happened, ever, and I didn't. I don't know why I did it, but I saw one of the brand-new pacifiers my mother had bought—unwrapped on the bottom shelf of the baby bassinet—and I took it. It was small and red, and I popped it in my mouth. It tasted awful, rubbery and dry. The little nipple was small. It didn't quite fit, but I kept it there and I sucked on it. No one was listening to me anyway.

"Oh, my goodness, Don, look. Look at Leah," my mother said.

My dad put down the camera. He put his arm around my mom, and they both stood there, thinking I was so cute—but I don't remember ever hurting as much as I did right at that moment.

Nineteen

Where were you, Dad? It was a Saturday. Where were you?

What was the truth?

Maggie stood looking at her father. The truth was her dad wasn't there because he had moved out three weeks before. They had separated. It was Saturday, and their mom was trying to get her errands done before she had to go to work. She left them in the house alone, and all they had to do was stay inside.

"Maggie, it's going to be all right. You're going to be all right," he said. "We both love you. That will never change."

What was the truth? Was it the memory? If you don't take a movie of it, a video, a photo — if it isn't recorded — is it then forever lost to interpretation, to human error? And what if you had? What if you could see a movie? Would that make it any more truthful?

When Maggie closed her eyes, she could see her sister under the water, looking up, pleading. What was she trying to say?

"I *was* there, Daddy."

The truth is not a single thing, word, event. Memory is more ephemeral than time. It is, by definition, only as valid as its intention—which isn't saying very much at all. And that was the moment Mrs. Paris decided to walk into the room.

"What do you mean, Maggie?" she asked.

Maggie didn't answer. She thought she could still smell Matthew on her clothing. She remembered how lonely, how lost, she'd felt when he thrust up against her and how badly she had longed to be with Nathan then. Right now, knowing she had ruined it, lost it all, gotten just what she deserved, it felt just right. Or if not *just right,* well, then, inevitable.

"I was there." Maggie turned to her mother. "We went to the pool together that morning. It was so hot inside."

"No," Mrs. Paris said. "You are wrong. I saw you. I saw you show up. You heard the sirens. You were alone. You came later, Maggie. You came when it was all over."

Maggie watched her mother's tortured face twist back through the years that had never passed the way ordinary time is supposed to pass. Certain measures of time don't move at all.

"I think you *think* you were there, Maggie,"

Mr. Paris said. He kept his hands on the kitchen table, crossing and then recrossing his clasped fingers. "We talked about it so much then. You must have heard us. We tried not to talk in front of you, but the doctors . . . Grandma . . . and all the neighbors . . . those three days when Leah was in the hospital."

"You can't remember. You were too little. You were too young," Mrs. Paris said, because it was easier for her that way. "You don't remember anything, Maggie."

"I do," Maggie said. "I was there. I watched her die, Daddy. And I left. I ran for help. I ran to find you, Mommy."

Mrs. Paris made some kind of noise, though Maggie couldn't say for sure whether it had come from her mother's mouth or directly from her broken heart. But it was the sound truth makes when it doesn't have anyplace left to go, when it forces its way to the surface.

Maggie begged Nathan to come over, just to listen. Just to come over. Even to yell at her. But he would do none of those things.

"Why did you even tell me?" he asked her on the phone.

Maggie was sobbing. "I don't know. I don't know."

She wanted his forgiveness. She wanted to have done something really terrible and still be loved.

"I can't, Maggie. I can't even listen to this."

But she wanted him to know and she told him everything. About the car and the parking lot and how awful she felt. "Please just talk to me. Please don't do this to me."

"To you, Maggie?" Nathan's voice was stiff. It was distant and hard. "It's always about you."

"Please, please, just come over," she pleaded.

"No," he said. He reminded her, "I don't sell a good thing twice."

Lucas and Dylan came home that night. They had no idea of anything that had transpired, and somehow that made it easier for everyone to put it aside, as if just as they walked in the door, having been dropped off by Grandma, the talking stopped.

It picked up in bits and pieces over the weeks to come, the next months and years after, but Mr. and Mrs. Paris remained separated, and eventually one of them filed for divorce, though Maggie never found out which one.

That night, after Mrs. Paris got the boys to bed, after Maggie tried and failed to make Nathan love her, even *speak* to her, again, after her dad had driven off, but not before packing up another box or two of his belongings, Maggie's mother came into her room.

"It was my fault, Maggie, and no one else's," she said. She sat on the end of the bed, facing the wall, talking into the darkness. "What kind of mother leaves her kids alone and goes shopping?"

It wasn't a question, of course. "Leah was always naughty. Always rebellious. There wasn't a rule she didn't want to break."

Maggie thought she could see a breeze that day, a hot summer breeze blowing her mother's hair. Her daughter standing on the other side of the fence, watching it all in horror.

"I was just so tired. And Leah was such a handful in the grocery store. She wanted everything. She fought me on everything." Mrs. Paris turned to Maggie. "And you were easy. You were always the easy one."

Tears formed inside her mother's eyes and filled them until it seemed to Maggie that no eyes could hold so much water.

"That morning. I don't know if you remember. I wanted to take you both. You were all dressed and ready, but Leah was having a tantrum about what she would wear. She said she had no nice clothes like everyone else had. She hated everything she owned. So she stomped into her room and pulled out everything from her drawers and dumped it on the floor. Do you remember that?"

Maggie shook her head. She knew that she and Leah shared a room back in that condo, but she had no memory of the clothing, the empty drawers, or the tantrum.

"There were clothes everywhere. She had even pulled her good dresses from their hangers, and I had just spent the whole morning cleaning. I was tired, Maggie. I was so tired. Anyway," Mrs. Paris continued, "I told Leah to stay inside. I told her she couldn't come with us, then."

"Us?"

Mrs. Paris let her head nod up and down very slowly. "Yeah, I took your hand. I said, 'OK, then. I'll take Maggie. I'll take my *good* daughter.'"

The water spilled over in ripples and waves and floods that would never end. "But you wouldn't go. You wouldn't leave your sister. You begged me to wait. You told me *you'd* clean up the mess. You wouldn't go; I couldn't believe it. You were my good one. I didn't have the strength to fight, so just I left. I left you both."

"Well, I guess you were wrong about that," Maggie said after a beat.

"What do you mean? Other than everything."

"That I was the good one. Now you know. I was sure not the good one."

"Oh, Maggie. I'm so sorry. You'll never know how sorry I am." Mrs. Paris spoke the truth, like filling a bottomless well.

Then Maggie said, after a long beat, "Mom, Nathan broke up with me," and she started to cry from a depth that she could only begin to measure. Mrs. Paris put her arm around her daughter, and they stayed that way for a long time.

Leah

Maggie? Maggie, if I could say one last thing? If I could tell you not to blame yourself. If I could tell you how it all turns out in the end —

You know I am sorry that you lost your boyfriend and that ten years from now, when you show up at the church on Old Main Street at noon, he won't be there.

He seemed like a really nice guy. He is a nice guy, and you will always have that memory. No one ever forgets their first love, and you are lucky it was such a positive experience. It might not feel that way now, but you are very lucky for that.

And I know you are sorry for the way you treated him, and he will always have that pain, even when it becomes just another story. For both of you.

Like the love we had for each other, and the love we will always have for each other. Because you know what they say—love never dies. It never really dies, Maggie. Little baby Gwen.

Little Maggie.

And I'm real sorry about Mom and Dad. But their story began long before either one of us came along. They couldn't work it out, not then and not now, and there was nothing we could do about that. It's their crap, Maggie, not ours.

But if I could be the one to ease your mind (forgive yourself) and heal your body (take care of it; guard it more closely) and tell you how wonderful you truly are, tell you how wonderful the life you have ahead of you will be—

If I could—

I would, little sister.

Believe me, I surely would.

But this is your journey now, and yours alone.

It's going to be OK, Maggie. It's all going to be all right.

Thank you

To Deb Noyes Wayshak, gifted writer and shrewd editor, who read many painful drafts of this story before she kindly and wisely suggested I go back to the source and trust myself again.

To Hannah Mahoney and Kate Herrmann, the most perfect copy editors any writer could ask for, and for proofreader extrordinaire, Martha Dwyer. I know I didn't make it easy.

To my wonderful literary agents, Nancy Gallt and Marietta Zacker.

To Dal Lowenbein for allowing me to call her up at any hour and ask her things like, "Now, if your sister were drowning . . . "

And as always, to my Children's Authors who Breakfast at the Bluebird in Easton, CT, Tony Abbot and Elise Broach (They even helped me with these acknowledgments!)—what would I do without you guys?

To Lauren Border, who patiently answered all my girls' swim team questions and who was, coincidentally, my very first creative writing student, so very long ago.

To my (grown) boys (both writers themselves), Sam and Ben, always and forever.